# THE ROSE KILLER

**GARY PEARSON**

Copyright © 2020 by Gary Pearson

All rights reserved.

No part of this book may be reproduced in any form or by any electronic or mechanical means, including information storage and retrieval systems, without written permission from the author, except for the use of brief quotations in a book review.

Published: 28th September 2018

This novel is entirely a work of fiction. The names, characters and incidents portrayed in it are the work of the author's imagination. Any resemblance to actual persons, living or dead, events, or locales is entirely coincidental.

Gary Pearson asserts the right to be identified as the author of this work.

Text Copyright © 2016 Gary Pearson

Cover Art Copyright © 2016 MD Design

The right of Gary Pearson to be identified as an author has been asserted by him in the accordance with the Copyright, Designs and Patents Act 1988.

Second Edition.

# CONTENTS

| | |
|---|---|
| Acknowledgments | v |
| ONE | 1 |
| TWO | 8 |
| THREE | 15 |
| FOUR | 18 |
| FIVE | 23 |
| SIX | 28 |
| SEVEN | 33 |
| EIGHT | 37 |
| NINE | 43 |
| TEN | 50 |
| ELEVEN | 53 |
| TWELVE | 60 |
| THIRTEEN | 64 |
| FOURTEEN | 70 |
| FIFTEEN | 74 |
| SIXTEEN | 84 |
| SEVENTEEN | 87 |
| EIGHTEEN | 91 |
| NINETEEN | 97 |
| TWENTY | 103 |
| TWENTY-ONE | 111 |
| TWENTY-TWO | 114 |
| TWENTY-THREE | 118 |
| TWENTY-FOUR | 125 |
| The Highwayman | 129 |
| ONE | 130 |
| Also by Gary Pearson | 133 |
| About the Author | 135 |

## ACKNOWLEDGMENTS

I would like to thank everyone for their support and belief in me during my time writing this; you know who you are, and without you, I would not have gotten this far.
To my love, you have pushed me onwards and upwards with my writing, helping to give me the time I need and encouragement to get this out there so that people can read it.
Also I want to thank the likes of James Patterson, Lee Child, Terry Pratchett, and more recently Michael Connelly, for opening my eyes to the world of reading from a younger age and allowing me to delve into their worlds, which in turn gave me inspiration to get into writing in the first place.

# ONE

**CHICAGO, ILLINOIS**
**NOVEMBER, 1954**

The Ford Mainline turned onto West 17th Street and gently ground to a halt. The driver killed the engine, grabbed his grey fedora off the passenger seat, and then exited the car. Detective Ian Harlow stepped out into the dark silent night.

He pulled the collar up on his coat and placed the hat on his head to shield him from the cold, his breath clouding in front of him. No matter how long a person lives in Chicago, and no matter how accustomed they become, it was always painfully cold in the winter. He stepped around the car, and headed across the street towards the alley. There was a cop standing in front of some yellow crime scene tape that stretched across the entrance. It whipped on the wind, breaking the dull silence. He pulled his badge out of his pocket and held it up to the man, who nodded, and Harlow ducked beneath the tape. As he neared the volley of people in front of him, he pulled a pack of Chesterfields out of his pocket, tapped one into his hand, struck a match, and lit the cigarette, taking a long drag on it.

"Talk to me, Charlie," he said to his partner, Charlie Garroway, who was knelt on the ground by the body. He blew out a lungful of purple smoke.

"Female. Twenty-eight. Cause of death; my guess is strangulation."

Harlow nodded slowly as he glanced down at the body. He could see the deep purple marks that laced the neckline of the victim. He looked over the rest of the body laid before him and frowned. In her outstretched hand was a single stemmed red rose.

"Shit," he said slowly.

"You noticed that, huh?" Garroway commented, gesturing towards the rose. "Looks like our man is back."

"It's been eight months, Charlie. Why now?"

"Your guess is as good as mine."

"Any connection to the other girls?"

"None that we can see. Other than the fact she's female, attractive and blonde."

The last three years had been a cat and mouse chase for Harlow. He'd been trying to track down the notorious Rose Killer, a demented serial killer that left a single stemmed red rose at the scene of every murder. Now, including this one tonight, his total was up to eighteen.

Harlow had gotten close once, so close, and nearly caught the guy in the act, but he had gotten away and left a bullet hole in Harlow's shoulder, and a bigger hole in his pride. Many man-hours had been ploughed into trying to find the killer. Eight months of nothing, nada, zip, and now another body turns up on the street. There was no connection between any of the victims, other than the fact that they were attractive, female, and all blonde. Everything else was a complete mystery.

"We know anything about her?" Harlow asked.

"Her name was Casey Greenway."

Harlow nodded. "Anything else?"

"Not really. We found this on her."

Garroway held up a white matchbook. Etched on the front in black writing was the word, *Minkys*.

"The bar up on Rush Street?" Harlow queried.

"The very same."

For the first time that night, Harlow smiled, "So let's go have a look around."

---

Fifteen minutes later, Harlow and Garroway pulled up opposite Minky's bar on Rush Street. The thoroughfare was bustling with busy people, despite the late hour. As they got out of the car and headed towards the door, they saw a poster on the wall.

"I think that answers our question of what she was doing in here," Harlow said as he gestured towards the poster. It showed a list of entertainers that sang every night at the bar during their long, various hours.

One of the names on the list was Casey Greenway.

As they entered the bar, the haze of cigarette smoke was hanging in the air, like an early morning fog. Harlow instinctively lit up another one to contribute to the mist, and they walked to the bar. There was a woman on the stage, singing a slow melody along to the jazz band behind her. The people sitting at the tables seemed to be enjoying themselves, smiling and joking. Whether they were actually paying attention to her was another story.

"Can I get you boys a drink?" The barman asked as they reached him.

"No thanks," Harlow said, as he held out his badge. "I'm Detective Harlow, this is my partner Detective Garroway."

"How can I help you?"

"There a manager around that I can speak to?"

"Yeah, he's just over there."

The barman gestured towards a table in front of the stage, just off to the left hand side. Harlow nodded once, turned, and walked over.

As he approached the table, he noticed a middle-aged man sitting with a woman on either side of him. Both of them were giggling and whispering things into his ear.

"You the manager?" Harlow asked on approach.

The man gazed up at him. Harlow flashed his badge.

"Depends on what you're here for?" the man replied.

"I'm Detective Harlow. This is my partner Detective Garroway. We need to ask you a few questions about Casey Greenway."

The man stopped laughing at what one of the women was saying into his ear. He beckoned for them both to leave. They stood up reluctantly, and simultaneously walked away, glaring at Harlow as they left, like he had ruined their evening. The man put his hand out and asked the detectives to sit.

"Jimmy Train," he said.

"Mr Train…" Harlow started.

"Please," he interrupted. "Call me Jimmy. Don't nobody call me Mr Train around here, just sounds plain weird."

There was a hint of Texan in his deep voice. As the men sat down, they could see the full profile of Jimmy Train. He was indeed a middle-aged man, his hair slicked back with grease, and he wore a fine suit, one that was tailored to perfection.

"Forgive me for asking, but you're not from around here are you?" Harlow asked.

"Nah. I'm from the good ol' south. Born an' raised in Austin, Texas. My daddy moved us on up here when we were teenagers. He got a job up in the ol' Windy City. Been here ever since."

"Never lost your accent though, I notice."

"Some things never die," Jimmy said proudly.

"So it seems," Harlow said. "Anyway I'll get to the point. We're here investigating the murder of Casey Greenway…"

"Casey's … dead?" Jimmy slowly asked.

"I'm afraid so. We need to ask you a few questions about her, if that's okay?"

"Sure. Casey was a brilliant girl. Voice like an angel. She's the reason we sold out on so many nights, when she was playin'. Not sure what we're gonna do now, though."

"Do you know of anyone that would want to cause her any harm? Did she have any enemies, anyone that showed any signs of hostility towards her when she was here?"

"Don't be silly, she was loved by everyone. She was the kindest person I ever did know. She wouldn't say boo to a goose."

"Do you know of any reason someone would want to hurt her? Any jealous boyfriends or ex-lovers that may have been hanging around? I'm guessing if the girl was that good, she would've been getting a lot of attention too?"

"Yeah, that she did. The boys loved her; however, she made it very clear that she was not interested. They then kept themselves to themselves, respected her wishes, and she got on with her job."

"When did you last see Casey?"

"She performed earlier tonight, finished around seven. Left here about eight, I think."

"Any idea where she might have been going? Anything she said to you?"

"Nah, nothing. Just that she was going home. Nothin' else was said really. She used to keep herself to herself. I can't believe she's gone."

"You and me both, Jimmy. Do you have any contact details for Casey? Address, next of kin, those kinds of things?"

"Nah. Just had a number for her in case she didn't show up for work, but she always did, was always early too."

"Okay. Well thanks for your time, Jimmy, and I'm sorry for the inconvenience it'll cause you."

"Good luck finding the fella that did it. That SOB deserves to be buried for this."

"Indeed he does, Jimmy," Harlow said. "Indeed he does."

When they left the bar, Garroway turned; a question on his face. "That seem right to you, Ian? We go in there and tell him one of his best performers was murdered tonight, and he hardly reacts."

"He's pissed off cause he's now gotta find a new act to fill the slot. That's his only issue. He didn't care anything for her."

"That may be so, but if you came and told me one of my employees had died then I'd be a little more shook up than he was."

"Maybe you're right," Harlow agreed. "Why don't you stick around and keep an eye on our friend. I'm gonna head back to the department to see if I find out where she lived, or find any more information on her. I'll catch up with you later."

Charlie nodded and stepped back into the bar, leaving

Harlow out on the street. The cold air was biting at him now. He pulled his jacket tight around him and lit another cigarette, in an attempt to try to warm his insides. He took a long drag as he headed for the car, climbed in, and drove back towards the precinct.

## TWO

The late hour meant the precinct was practically empty, only a few people milled around doing some last-minute paperwork, and the rest were officers working the night shift. Harlow groaned at the lack of resources still within the office, he'd always been a dedicated workman, first in, last out, often doing far too much.

The room was a long space spanned by desks on either side. As he approached his own, near the back of the room, he saw that the desk light was on. When he reached it, his attention wary, there was a box laying on the top, with a single stemmed red rose pinned to it. Harlow looked around the office slowly, alert, seeing if anyone was watching for when he arrived at his desk. He lifted the lid; inside sat the tip of a severed finger. Looking closer he could see that it belonged to a women, it was slim, and the nail had previously been painted with dark colouring, red, which had started to chip away. The only other thing inside was a piece of paper neatly folded. He paused, breathed in, opened the letter, and read:

. . .

*Detective Harlow,*

*I hope you have been keeping well, and that your shoulder has now fully healed. I do feel slightly bad for that.*

*We have played this game for a long time now, and I am disappointed that you still have not found me. I thought I had given you enough opportunity in the past. Clearly, I need to be more obvious for you. You see, despite everything, I admire you. I think you are a brilliant detective that doesn't get enough recognition. I know that, as you near the end of your career, you would like to be the person that was known for catching the great Rose Killer. It seems to roll off the tongue that saying. So, I am going to give you the chance. I want to see how good you really are. I know that you will be reading this tonight, probably after you visited the whore's workplace. So, I am telling you that, tomorrow at midday, there will be another body. The gift inside this box should hopefully prove that I mean serious business.*

*I hope to see you soon,*
*Your friend,*
*The Rose Killer.*


Harlow's hand was shaking by the time he placed the letter back onto his desk, not from fear but from the brewing anger that was raging within him.

The nerve! The fact the killer had the balls to come into *his* precinct and place this on *his* desk was infuriating.

He pulled a cigarette out of his packet, his fingers trembling, and lit it, inhaling the fumes, and felt the anger slowly subside. He walked over to the counter, to speak to the night clerk.

"David," Harlow asked. "Did anyone bring anything in for me this evening?"

The man's eyes darted from left to right as he tried to recount everyone that he had seen or spoken to since the shift started. Eventually he shook his head, a firm no.

"No one at all? No messages left for me?"

The clerk looked down at his desk. "Not that I can see. No one has asked me to give you anything."

Harlow went back to his desk, replaced the lid on the box, and grabbed the letter. He walked back out of the department and got into his car, racing back towards Minky's.

As he screeched to a halt outside, he climbed out, picking up the letter as he went, and headed in through the doors. He noticed Garroway at the bar and headed over to him.

"Couldn't stay away, huh?" Garroway said.

"This fucker had the audacity to do *this*," Harlow said, thrusting the letter towards Garroway's chest.

He read it, curious. When Garroway hit a certain part of the page, his face went white. He slowly looked up at Harlow with his mouth hanging open.

"This … this came for you?" he stuttered.

"Came for me? It was in the office on *my* desk. Sent with a rose, of course."

"But how did he … when did he…?"

"I don't know. Not quite worked that one out yet. All I know is we've gotta try and keep this next person alive. Whoever it may be."

"Did he leave any clues? Any other information?"

"Nothing. Just the severed finger. I'd send it to be finger printed, but we wouldn't get the results back by midday."

"True. Well, we'll put a call out to all units to find out if anyone has been reported missing."

"The only problem is a lot of people have been reported as missing recently. We'd be lucky to find a match."

"We don't know if we don't try, Ian."

"True. Well, let's make the call to missing persons, and see if we can get anything back. In the meantime, let's head to the precinct and see if we can get anything from that letter."

Both of the men walked out of the bar, got into the car, and headed south towards the precinct.

As they pulled up to the curb outside, Chief Stammerwood was standing outside patiently, waiting for them.

"Evening, chief," Harlow said as he exited the vehicle. "What are you doing out here?"

"Waiting for your sorry asses. We've got ourselves a situation."

Harlow and Garroway glanced at one other, confused as to whether the chief knew about the finger already, or if this was something completely new.

"I think you two better come with me," the chief said, solemnly.

As they entered the department, the few people that were still on duty all stopped what they were doing, and looked up at the three new arrivals. All of them had the same worried expression on their faces. As they went in through the door to the chief's office, he shut it behind them and gestured for them to sit.

Harlow took his hat off, removed his coat, and pulled out the old wooden chair before him. It creaked as he sat down. Garroway pulled one out alongside him and followed suit. The chief walked around to the other side of his desk, and exhaled as he sat.

He lit a cigarette, picked up a piece of paper from his desk, and slowly blew smoke out of his nostrils.

"Gentlemen. We have a situation."

"You said, chief. We kind of already have one of our own."

"You can forget everything you're doing right now, and focus all of your attention on this shit storm."

He slid a letter across the desk, which settled perfectly in front of Harlow. He picked it up and held it so that his partner could also read it at the same time.

*Chief Stammerwood,*

*Firstly, I would like to say what a wonderful job you have done for the city of Chicago in the last fifteen years. The streets have never felt safer, other than the fact that you have never been able to catch me, of course.*

*The press have labelled me The Rose Killer, and I'll be honest, I quite like the name. When I set out on this journey, I never expected to become so notorious. You have been chasing me for the last three years and still nothing. Detective Harlow has been doing a sterling job, but I feel he and your department needs a bit more inspiration in the race to catch me. So, I will inform you that a body will turn up on your streets everyday until you finally catch me. I started this evening, which Detective Harlow is already looking into. I already pre-warned him, and gave him ample inspiration by sending him a souvenir from my next victim.*

*If you do not start to take me seriously then your whole department shall be exploited for the shambles that it obviously is.*

*Yours,*
*The Rose Killer.*

"Where did this come from?" Harlow asked, as he finished reading.

"It was delivered to my fucking house," Stammerwood replied. "What does he mean when he says he's already given you some inspiration?"

"Well, this is what I meant by we have a situation of our own. We found a body on the street earlier today, the usual M.O. Female, blonde, strangled to death, and a single stemmed red rose. It's the first that's come up in eight months. We went to where she worked, to try and find some information on her. When I came back to the office there was a box on my desk with a rose on top. When I opened it, there was a letter addressed to me, and a severed finger inside."

"A finger?" the chief asked.

"Yes. The killer claims that it's from his next victim, which will turn up at midday tomorrow unless I can find him first. He's toying with me, trying to get me to go after him."

"Which is *exactly* what you should be doing! We can't afford to start having a body turn up on a daily basis. Do you know what the press will do to us? I already have the Tribune breathing down my neck about this killer. You need to get your asses out there and find this guy. I don't care how you do it, just find him!"

"With all due respect, chief, how do you know it's a him?" Garroway asked.

Both Harlow and Stammerwood looked at each other for a brief moment, before turning their attention towards Garroway.

Stammerwood laughed, incredulously. "You think some *broad* is out there killing her own kind? Don't be stupid."

"You don't know what some people are capable of, chief," Harlow butted in.

The chief sighed. "Fine. Get out there and find out who he, or she is. If I have to answer to the higher powers as to why we've not caught this person, believe me, you will be answering to me personally. Do I make myself clear?"

"Very," Harlow said.

He stood up and placed his fedora back onto his head, draped his coat over his arm, and walked out of the office.

# THREE

Harlow placed his hat on the rack, sat down at his desk, moved the mountains of paperwork to one side, and leant back. He linked his fingers together behind his head, and stared up at the ceiling. Garroway sat down on the opposite side of the desk, and exhaled.

"What happens now?"

Harlow narrowed his eyes. "Now we catch the bad guy. That's the only option we have. This shit has gotten very serious, very quickly. For some unknown reason, it seems like he's got a personal vendetta against me."

Garroway nodded slowly.

"He's never come after you in any way before. I don't know why he's decided to now."

"He's sent me two messages. The first is the finger in the box. The second was in the message to the chief. What we need to figure out is why. Why is he targeting me?"

"That's the million dollar question, Ian. If we knew that, the case would be closed already."

Harlow nodded at the thought, then moved and pulled the box in front of him. He removed the rose from the top and lifted the lid. Grabbing a piece of paper off the desk, he lifted the finger out. He moved it around, looking at the edges of it.

"Look at this." He pushed it towards Garroway. "Looks like the finger was hacked off, that's not a clean cut. The person this was removed from would have suffered, and my guess is they would've been alive during the process."

Garroway leant forward and peered at the finger held within the paper. He stared at the ragged edges of the severed end, where it had been cut from the rest of the hand.

"My guess would be a hacksaw of some kind. Look at the damage to the skin. It's the kind of mark you would get from raking it across," Garroway said, making the motion with his outstretched palm.

"Poor bitch," Harlow retorted. "Take it to be finger printed. See if we can get any information from it."

Garroway folded the paper around the finger, took it from Harlow, and stood up.

"Tell them it's urgent. We need the results yesterday," Harlow called, as Garroway walked away.

"Will do, Ian. I'll stay down with them and see if I can do anything to speed the process up."

"Good idea. Let me know when you've got something."

Garroway raised his hand in acknowledgment as he disappeared out of the room. Harlow sat staring at the box on his desk. He put his hands in and moved the shredded paper around that had been sitting in the base. With the realisation that nothing else remained in there, he chucked it down on the floor.

"Why aren't you doing anything, Harlow? *What did I tell you?*" Stammerwood bellowed across the vast room.

"Just getting started, chief."

"Started. You should've finished by now!"

Harlow stood up, sighed, walked down past his chief, and made his way to the exit.

"Where are you going?" Stammerwood asked.

"To the file room. I'm gonna have to dig through all of the stuff we have on this sonofabitch to see if something's been missed in the past."

"At least I'll know where to find you if I need you, but you need to get a move on. You've got just over twelve hours until the next body apparently shows up. And I'll be damned if I'm having another letter come to my home, or body part coming into this office."

"Gotcha, chief. I'll find this bastard. You have my word."

"Your word better be good enough."

"He's made it personal now. He's questioned my ability and that of our entire precinct. I'll show him what the Chicago PD will do to him."

"That's the right attitude to have. Let's hope we can do this and get him before too many bodies show up on the street."

"I'll do my best, chief."

"You catch this bastard by any means necessary, you hear me? If you need another cop or two, to help out or something, just tell them. If they try and get funny, then send them my way. We all need to work together as a team on this one. This guy has gone way past the line."

"Agreed. I'll let you know when I come up with something."

The chief nodded once, and Harlow headed out of the room, down the stairs towards the file room.

# FOUR

As Harlow entered the box room in the basement of the precinct, he looked around at the rows of filing cabinets lining the walls. Each of the brown metal cabinets housed mass paperwork of open or closed cases. He chucked his coat down on one of the chairs and placed his hat on the table. He knew instinctively which file to look for, which ones held the details of the killers. It was almost routine; he'd looked at them so many times in the past three years that it was second nature.

He walked over to the filing cabinet, opened it, and removed the dog-eared file. He chucked it down onto the table, the thick folder making a loud thump. He switched a small metal desk lamp on next to him, and pulled out a cigarette to help him through the beginning of the reading process.

He leafed through the file, pulling out the pictures of all of the victims that had succumbed to the killer over the years. He removed all seventeen pictures and moved them into a line on the table before him; faces of dead women were all that glared back at him.

They were all blonde, all attractive. Other than that, there was absolutely nothing that linked them all together. He stared at each one for a long minute, taking it in turns to study as much of their faces as he could. It was almost like he was trying to play a sadistic spot the difference with the pictures. None of them changed, all of their faces were in the same transfixed expression, and none of them looked like they were in pain, just in peace.

Almost like they knew what was going to happen before it did.

*Was this what he did?*

*Did he make them come to terms with what was about to happen to them? No, that can't be it. If you tell someone they're going to die they aren't going to be happy with it, they are going to want to fight, to run away, to call for help, something. Fight or flight.*

None of these women suffered any other pain; they were strangled to death, and the same bruising purple marks were always visible around the neck. After the autopsies had come back, there were no other injuries to report. By all accounts, most of them seemed to be in good health when they had died.

*So how did you manage to get to them, and kill them, without the victims suffering any other injuries? You would have done it from the front as the marks were always in the same spot. They would've seen you coming. Why did none of them try to run?*

His thoughts went around in circles for the next twenty minutes; during this time he ploughed through four cigarettes and was now starting to run low. He stubbed out his latest and leant back in his chair; he covered his face with his hands and slowly spoke to himself.

"Why are you doing this? What can I do to stop you? What do you want from me?"

"They are the exact questions that you need to answer, and quickly," a voice said, coming from behind him.

Harlow removed his hands from his face and looked up at the figure standing in the doorway. "Hi, Charlie," he said to his partner. "How did you get on with the prints?"

"They're doing it as we speak. They're not happy, but doing it nonetheless."

"Well that's something, I guess."

"How are you getting on down here?"

"Nothing links these girls, Charlie, nothing. The only thing they have in common is that they are all the same kind of age, and that they are all blonde. None of them knew each other, lived near each other, or had anyone in common. So how the hell does he pick his victims?"

"Ian, you might need to try and get some rest. You had a long day before this even started."

"Are you kidding? If I leave and go home now, the chief will have my ass. Hell, he'll probably have both our asses for not doing anything. You heard him earlier; we need to do what we can to catch this bastard."

"I know. But maybe you need to come back and look at all this with fresh eyes, in the morning."

"If I come back in the morning, without having gotten closer to finding him, then another girl will turn up dead. That'll be on me."

"No. That'll be on him, Ian. You can't fight this guy. You got close once and almost got yourself killed. You remember that night, right?"

"Of course I remember it. I wake up in the night because of it. But that day, I got lucky. I happened to be in the area when it happened. You know that."

"I do. We found out that day that the guy carries a Beretta around with him, ballistics from the bullet that came out of your shoulder told us that."

Harlow rubbed his hand over the scar from the old wound; every now and then, it ached, especially when he was thinking about it. Then he stopped, as if a bolt of lightning had struck him.

"Charlie, why does this guy carry a Beretta with him? If all he does is strangle the women, and then leaves them for someone to find, why carry the gun?"

"In case one of them gives him a problem?" Garroway replied.

"Exactly, but none of these girls have been shot, all of them have been strangled."

"So what are you saying?"

"I'm saying that there might be more bodies out there that were killed by a gunshot wound, bodies of the victims that tried to get away, maybe they even managed to cause him a bit of pain. Either way, we would've overlooked them as a different murderer, or a one-off crime, not associated with the Rose Killer at all. Especially if none of them had a rose on them when the body was found."

"That's true. We only link all of these together because of the way they were killed, and the fact that he leaves the rose behind for us to find."

"Exactly. If this is all some weird plan that he had, and he wants it to be perfect, then he would not tarnish it by leaving a victim that was shot for us to find. It wouldn't look right. Get some boys down here; we need to go through these files and find any homicides that were committed with a Beretta. The victim needs to be a female, around the same kind of ages as these, and they need to have blonde hair. We need to look for the same victim type, same M.O., but killed by a specific gun instead, no strangulation. Shouldn't be too hard to find."

"There's got to be hundreds of cases like that. We'll be here for hours."

Harlow shot him a look.

"I'll get right on it," Charlie said, heading back out of the door and away up the stairs.

"I've got you now, you bastard," Harlow said, grinning.

# FIVE

Chief Stammerwood came down into the filing room an hour later. There were three men sitting around the big desk with a large stack of files in front of them, each one taking a document from the top, leafing through it, and either tossing it to one side, or placing it in a different pile.

"Mind telling me what's going on down here, Harlow?"

"Something came to me earlier, whilst I was talking with Charlie. The night I almost caught him and got shot."

"We all remember that well. You were lucky to escape alive," Stammerwood interjected.

"That may be so, but it got me thinking. Why does he need a gun when all he does is strangle the girls? Therefore, I've got the guys down here trying to find victims of the same description as his usual ones, but killed by a Beretta instead. In theory, we might stumble across his failures."

"How are they failures if he killed them anyway?"

"I think all of this is some kind of huge, perfect plan that he has in his head. He would have been meticulously organising it for years, and has spent the last three exercising it. Until now. Now, he has decided to announce himself, more personally than ever before. He has contacted you and me directly, saying that he wants me to catch him. Why? Why would any rightful criminal want to get caught? Especially when he has committed so many murders, and knows he will probably get the death sentence for it."

"I don't know," Stammerwood said.

"Neither do I, that's the part that I'm trying to figure out. Before that, I want to know if there are other murders out there that we might have missed, crimes we assumed, at the time, were committed by somebody else. There may be more clues in these files that could potentially lead us back to him."

"Good thinking, Harlow, I'll give you that. Shame you didn't come up with it before now, though. Just do what you need to do to find him, and quickly."

---

As the first light of the day started to thread its way through the blinds, Harlow sat at his desk going through a bundle of files and pictures. He had dragged himself away from the dark room in the early hours of the morning, to get some coffee, and had found his old chair more comfortable than the ones in the file room, so stayed there. He had searched through what felt like hundreds of cases in the space of the last few hours. Other officers had also done the same, in an attempt to find some connections. Chief Stammerwood appeared in front of his desk, just twenty minutes later.

"Did you find anything?" he asked.

"Yeah a lot," Harlow responded.

"Anything that we can actually go on?"

"The guys are still going through the files as we speak."

"Are you any closer to finding him?"

"Probably closer than I was last night, before I started all of this."

"Are we going to catch this guy before a body turns up at midday?"

"That I can't tell you, chief."

"I told you that we need to find this guy. I can't start having bodies turning up on the streets, and this guy taunting us saying that we are all poor at our jobs. The commissioners won't stand for it."

"Tell me something I don't know," Harlow growled. "I wanna find this guy just as much, and if not, more than you do. He's come out and challenged me specifically, delivered a body part to *my* desk, no one else's. He has a vendetta against me not you, and not the rest of the department. For some reason he thinks it should be me that catches him. Why he wants to be caught is still beyond me, and I don't know why. If you think you are that good at something, why would you want to be caught?"

"You've got half an hour. I want some news by then. We're expecting a body, so I want to give the commissioner a heads up."

"Fine. I will bring you what I have then."

As Stammerwood walked away, Garroway walked into the room. He had just come in from outside, and the cold was leaking off of him. It made Harlow shiver slightly.

"Jesus, Ian. You even slept?"

Harlow shook his head.

"You haven't even been home yet, have you?" Garroway remarked, whilst noticing that Harlow was still wearing the same clothes from the night before.

"I told you last night. If I go home, I won't sleep anyway. My time was better put to use here, trying to find some information. Just as yours should have been. Where did you go?"

"I went home, Ian. Which is where you should've gone. You should've made the guys sift through all of that shit last night and gotten some sleep. You're no good to anyone when you're running on fumes."

"I'm fine," Harlow replied, whilst draining the final dregs of his now cold coffee, and lighting another cigarette.

"I take that back. Running on caffeine and nicotine. Well, have you managed to get anywhere?"

"The guys are just finishing up as we speak. We found a load of cases that had the right victims but not the right gun, or vice versa. There are some there though, that could be our guy."

"So you think it's definitely a guy?"

"You were the one that raised the sex of the person. I think there's a seventy per cent chance that it's a guy, purely because I think the person that attacked me that night was a guy. Not many women out there would have handled that pistol the way that the killer did."

"They didn't finish the job though. You're still here, after all."

"I know. Lucky, I guess."

"Or maybe they didn't want to kill you. Maybe the killer was leading up to this moment. The moment where they could challenge you."

"Is that what you think this is? A challenge?"

"Don't you? They've called you out by name. They've asked you to catch them. In my eyes, that's a challenge. Let's hope that you're up to it."

Harlow leapt up off his chair, grabbed Garroway by the collar, and pulled him in close. "Don't question my integrity or what I'm capable of. I'll find this fucker," he said angrily.

"Okay, Ian. I didn't mean anything by it. I was just saying … well it doesn't matter. I'm sorry."

Harlow let go of Garroway's jacket, and sat back down in his chair. He took a drag on his cigarette as Garroway readjusted himself.

"We've gotta go and see the chief in just over twenty minutes, to go through what we know. Go and see if the boys downstairs have finished and bring up all of the intel they have for me, will you?"

"Sure thing, Ian."

Harlow got up out of his chair and walked over to the coffee pot, which had been recently refilled, and poured himself another cup. The coffee at the station always tasted like shit but it was strong enough to keep him awake, and right now, that was what he needed more than anything else.

## SIX

Garroway arrived back at his desk fifteen minutes later with a stack of twelve files. As he dropped the folders onto the desk, he pulled up a chair opposite.

"This is what the guys have found. All of the victims were female, blonde, around mid to late twenties, and were killed by a Beretta gunshot. As you said, all of the other victims were not as similar, had nothing in common with our guy's kills. Do you wanna go through them now?"

"Not enough time. We'll go through them with the chief. Hopefully, there's some information in there that we can use to try and hunt him down."

"It'll take days to dissect all of the information in these files, you know that right?"

"We need to get it done as soon as possible. We need to go through it all with a fine toothcomb."

"Like I said, it'll take us days."

"Well, we've got four hours until another body turns up on the street."

"Ian, we can't go through that amount of paperwork in

four hours. Not properly anyway, and not accurately, you know that."

"We need to do the best we can. Between you and me, I think that whatever happens, the body that is due to show up at midday is already dead."

"What makes you think that?"

"Because I don't think he would go to the effort of cutting a finger off a body that was still alive. I think that no matter what, we were meant to fail. Almost like we found him, but it was still too late, and the press will have a field day again."

"Maybe you're right, but what if you're wrong? We can't just give up hope of finding this girl."

"You're right. It's just a gut feeling I have. I've not given up complete hope that she's alive, whoever she is, but I think she's been dead for at least a day. The body would need to look fresh enough for us to think that it happened recently."

"You sound like you've *already* given up."

"As I said, it's a gut feeling. I've not completely given up. I just feel that she might be a wasted effort, and my main focus is trying to find him in general. Did you get anything from the missing persons department?"

"Nothing substantial. As we thought last night, the amount of woman with blonde hair in those age brackets, ones that go missing on a regular basis, is high. They are collating all of the cases reported in the last week. I should have them in the next hour."

"That might be too late. I wouldn't be surprised if some of the others were saved for future endeavours."

"You think he's collecting them?"

"You heard the chief's letter. One body will turn up everyday to prove how poor the department are. It seems strange he left that out of *my* letter, but I think he is collecting them, keeping them ready."

Garroway glanced at his watch. "Come on. We need to go and see the chief."

Harlow nodded as he stood up and grabbed the files from his desk. He walked across the space of the office, and rapped on the chief's door before letting himself in, without waiting for a response.

"Well?" Stammerwood said, as the two detectives walked into the office. "Tell me you're closer?"

"We've got twelve cases of murder where the victim matches his usual M.O., and were all killed with a Beretta," Harlow stated.

"And how does that help the poor little bitch that will turn up dead on our streets at midday?"

"It doesn't, chief, but it might help to eventually find the guy that's behind it all. I'm looking at the bigger picture here."

"The bigger picture? The bigger picture, *detective,* is that, at midday, the body of an innocent woman will be turning up on the street. Then another body a day until we catch this fucking guy. *That,* detective, is the bigger picture."

"If I'm honest, chief, I think the person will turn up dead today, no matter what happens. I think she's already dead."

"What you think and what is reality are two very different things."

"I understand that, but I think that she's already dead."

"*What* did I just say, detective? Do not assume anything. You will keep looking for this girl, right until it's too late, but not before. Do I make myself clear?"

"Yes, chief," Harlow said through gritted teeth.

"You say that you have twelve files. Are you any closer to knowing who this person is yet?"

"We've not had time to go through them fully –"

"What?" Stammerwood interrupted. "So let me get this

straight, you've been up all night, dragged pretty much the whole precinct down to the file room to assist you, and you've not had time to go through them? What the hell have you been doing down there?"

"I don't think you understand just exactly how many files are down there, chief. It's not the quickest archive to go through and then, when we find the files we need, we've then gotta go through those as well."

"I don't give a shit what your excuses are. You need to get as much on this fucker as possible, and get it now."

"Understood, chief."

"I have a meeting with the commissioner in the next hour. You need to have something for me by then."

"What if it's the same as what I've got for you now?"

"That's not an option. I can't go to the commissioner and tell him that a body will be turning up at midday, but we aren't going to bother looking for them because Detective Harlow *thinks* that they will already be dead, so there's no point."

Harlow looked away and off out of the window. The view of the city was beautiful, quaint, and silent. Despite the apprehension that dawned every time he stepped into Stammerwood's office, he always appreciated the view.

"Are you listening to me, Harlow?" Stammerwood barked.

"Loud and clear, chief."

"Then get off your ass, get back out there, and get me some information."

Both of the detectives stood up and left the office, heading back out into the precinct, which was slowly starting to fill up with the cops on their day shift. The officers that had been sifting through files of paperwork all night looked exhausted, and were glad to be going home.

"You think we can get any more information in the next hour?" Garroway asked, as they walked back to Harlow's desk.

"Doesn't look like we've got a choice. The chief wants someone's head for all this, and it looks like it's gonna be mine."

"It'll be ours, Ian. We're partners remember."

"Yeah. Well, somehow, I think you'll be okay. He seems to be laying all of this on me. Have you not noticed how he's not even directing any conversation at you?"

"Yeah, but I thought that's just because I keep quiet and don't say anything."

"There's more to it than that. It's because the letter that went to his house was about me, and the department. The box turned up on *my* desk, with the taunt aimed directly at me. He knows I have history with this guy. I'm the easy target if this all goes south."

"That may be, but I'd rather not take the risk. To be honest, if you go down then I think I'll be going down with you. Call it a gut feeling."

Garroway raised a wry smile, which Harlow simply snorted at. He lit a cigarette and grabbed the first file off the pile, and started to flick through the pages, seeing images, skimming words. Garroway sat on the other side of the desk and did the same. The next hour was going to be painful, and involve a lot of reading, despite Harlow's lack of sleep, but he needed to stay focused.

# SEVEN

As the end of the hour approached, the files on Harlow's desk had moved from one pile to the other. Both of the detectives looked tired and at the end of their tether. Harlow was flicking through his last one, knowing that he would soon be in front of Stammerwood, once more explaining that they still had nothing, and that the situation was exactly the same as what it was an hour earlier. Garroway suddenly slammed down his last file.

"You okay?" Harlow asked.

"There's nothing in these damn files, Ian. Not that we can see from looking through them so quickly. We know that all of the victims have a similar M.O., but this time killed with a Beretta and not strangled. Other than that, we are still in the same position we were earlier. Unless you've found something?"

"Not really," Harlow said, shaking his head slowly. "The only thing we might be able to use are potential locations. All of the files I've come across have all died within two blocks of Douglas Park, but that might just be coincidental. What about yours?"

Garroway picked up the first file and flicked through to a certain page. He put it down and moved on to the next, and so on, repeating the process until he had gone through all of them once more.

"Yeah, these are the same. Within two blocks of Douglas. That mean something to you?"

"Not a great deal. Where have the rest of the bodies been found? You know, the actual ones we know were killed by him?"

"I don't know, Ian. Not without going through all of the files for those. We don't have time for that."

"Maybe, but it might be something to go on. Even if we don't have time to go through it right now, it might be something that we can look through after the pointless meeting with the chief."

Garroway glanced down at his watch.

"Speaking of which, we need to get back in there."

Harlow nodded once, and then stood up. He grabbed a fresh cigarette, and filled his cup with the coffee from the pot, before heading across the precinct and into Stammerwood's office.

Stammerwood looked up. "About time. What have you got for me?"

"If I'm honest, chief, not a lot," Harlow responded.

"I told you I needed something within the hour. Are you that incompetent that you found out nothing?"

"We've come to the realisation that all of the killings in the files, the ones we dug up through the night, happened within two blocks of Douglas Park."

"Which means what to me? How is that any use?"

"It might mean that, if the other killings are within the same kind of radius, we might know roughly where the body might appear."

"So you're telling me that you want to scope out the area surrounding Douglas Park? And when I say area, I mean two blocks in every direction to see if a body may just turn up? Do you have any idea how many streets, alleyways, and other nooks and crannies are in that radius?"

"No, chief, but…"

"There are no *buts*, detective," Stammerwood interrupted. "I cannot go to the higher ups with that news. You've written this person off as being dead already."

"I think she's been dead for a couple of days."

The chief laughed. "And I told you that what you think, and what the truth is, are two very different things!"

Stammerwood's voice was raised now. Officers from the rest of the precinct turned towards the office, curious, looking to where the shouting was coming from.

"I will find him, chief. You know I will. I just need some more time."

"We don't have time. A body will turn up in four hours."

"I understand that, chief. Let me look through the other files on the killings we know he committed. I'll see if it matches up with my theory. Stall telling the commissioner. Hell, tell him when the body turns up that you received the note today for all I care. I just need more time."

"You've changed, detective. You would have never written someone off as being dead until they were lying there in front of you. I've known you to chase people up until it's been too late. What happened to you?"

Harlow said nothing.

"I asked you a question, *detective*."

Harlow paused for a beat, then said, "Nothing's changed chief. I just know for a fact that the girl that'll turn up today is dead. I don't wanna waste any time trying to find her when I need to look at the bigger picture, which is catching him."

He stubbed out his cigarette in the ashtray, stood up, and walked out of the office, leaving Garroway open mouthed in his wake.

# EIGHT

For the next three hours, Harlow and Garroway searched through the files. During this time they had the chief come and see them twice, hoping to get some kind of information. They made the decision to keep it from the commissioner, until a body appeared. It was not an easy decision but one that may save the lives of many other women. Sacrifice one for the sake of many. Harlow hated to admit it but it was the right choice. He knew that the body would turn up today, no matter what happened. It was probably already out there somewhere for all he knew, but what he did know was that he would do everything in his power to prevent any more deaths.

As the clock ticked into the eleventh hour of the day, Harlow stood up and headed for the exit.

"Where are you going?" Garroway asked, not looking up from the file he was reading.

"To get some fresh air. I've not left this place and seen the outside world in the last thirteen hours. That okay with you?"

Garroway looked a little surprised at Harlow's answer, but flashed him a slight smile anyway. Harlow walked past the rest of the officers and out into the day.

The cold was still there in all its force, the sun was out and there was not a cloud in the sky, but it felt like it was at least three below zero. He stretched his muscles and paced the outside of the station. He wanted to get a fresh pair of eyes on the files, and on the case in general. They had discovered the radius of the killings were all within two blocks of Douglas Park, they were sporadic, and in no particular direction, but all within two blocks. Harlow hated that he'd not discovered it previously, and that he'd noticed it now, when it was almost too late.

None of the bodies had shown up in the park, which was almost a little to strange for him to understand. He couldn't quite put his finger on why the Rose Killer liked to perform his kills around the area. He also didn't understand why all of the murders, strangled or otherwise, were committed at night, yet the killer had announced that the body would show up at midday today. There was also the question of how he would keep to schedule, how was he going to deliver a body at that time, and to where?

All of these were questions that would surely be answered soon enough.

Harlow looked at his watch. 11:15.

In forty-five minutes, he would have the answers to his questions. The chief had said that he would be sending cops out in all directions, two blocks out from the park. The problem with that was that some of the bodies showed up inside of the two blocks, so that theory was flawed, although he was happy for the chief to do it. Who knows, maybe they would get lucky.

That's what all of this boiled down to right now, luck.

If they got lucky, maybe one of the cops would see the killer delivering the body, or even killing the victim. Maybe, just maybe, the killer would fold, considering all of the police presence within his normal area, but these were all just guesses, and everything would have to align just right in order for one of those to happen.

As far as Harlow was concerned a body would show up at midday, they would do an autopsy on it a few days later, and the results would come in that she had been dead for a day or two before she had been found. It was out of character for the killer to do that, but then this whole game was out of character for him. He had never made contact before, and he had done so now, taunting him and the department for the fact that they had not yet caught him, and that they were incompetent.

This grated on Harlow more than anything else.

"I almost had you," Harlow growled to no one but himself. "You could have been taken care of a long time a go. You got lucky. Not me."

"Who are you talking to, Ian?"

The voice came from behind him, and Harlow spun to see who it was. His partner was standing there with a cup of coffee outstretched towards him.

"Thought you could use this whilst you were out here to get your senses back on track," he said.

"Thanks," Harlow replied.

"So, who were you talking to?"

"Myself. Just came to the realisation that I could've ended this a couple of years ago, when I almost caught him."

"Ian, you were lucky to get out of that situation *alive*."

"*No*. He's lucky to be out on the streets. *That's* what I've just come to terms with."

"He shot you, Ian."

"Yeah, but he didn't kill me. I've wondered for years whether he meant to miss, or whether he was just a poor shot. Seeing all of those victims in the files, where he had shot them, made me realise that he meant to keep me alive. That was the start of his game with me. A taunt that he could've killed me easily, but let me live. I see it the other way round though. I see it as I survived and he was lucky to still be out on the streets. If I hadn't been caught off guard, he would've been given the death penalty and it would've saved lives."

"Don't beat yourself up over it, Ian. If he'd killed you then you wouldn't be here today trying to stop him. You would've become another one of his victims."

"I know, but I didn't. Instead, he's now playing a game with me. Toying with me."

"Ian, come back down into reality. You're going to a dark place. You need some rest."

Harlow was pacing faster than before, gesturing with his hands as he spoke, as if all of this was coming to him for the first time. "He's gonna put on a show, and he's gonna unveil the body so that a lot of people see it, so that it shames the department for not catching him. He will want it in the Tribune. He loves the attention."

"Slow down, Ian. What are you saying?"

"I'm ... I'm not quite sure yet. It's my gut feeling again. I just think this is what the game is leading to."

Harlow seemed to have had an epiphany. It often came to him after a lack of sleep and copious amounts of coffee, and always during moments of high stress, in a wave. He could see everything clearer now, more than ever before. He realised that the killer loved the attention, loved the papers calling him The Rose Killer, loved the fact that the police had not yet caught him, and loved that he could now taunt them to try and catch him. He would now be staging more elaborate kills, maybe leading up to a grand finale.

"Ian? You still in there?" Garroway asked.

"Yeah, sorry. It's just come to me. I know what he wants."

Harlow said nothing else, and headed back into the precinct. He strode quickly through the desks, threading back to his own, and pulled a map of the city out of his drawer.

He unrolled it as he was moving things aside on his desk, to make room for it. He placed heavy objects on each of the corners, and grabbed a pen. Garroway had followed him back into the station and was now standing in front of the desk, looking confused.

"Charlie. Go through the files and tell me the locations of each of the murders."

Garroway picked up the first file and read off the body's location, then the second, and the third, and so on until all of the files had been recited. Each time, Harlow placed an X on the map. When it was a shooting, he marked it with a circle. When it was done, he stood back and lit a cigarette.

"Looks great but what does it mean?" Stammerwood appeared, staring at the map that was strewn across the desk.

"It's the locations of all of the murders," Harlow replied.

"Didn't we have something like this before?"

"Not with the shootings on, no."

Stammerwood leaned over and looked at the map.

"So, you were right that all of the murders took place within a two block radius of the park, but you still haven't given me any more information. There will be a body turning up in the next twenty minutes, for Christ's sake."

"Look at the crosses. Each of them are going round the park in a circular motion. The circles are in the exact place that I would expect the next body to be. It's almost as if he managed to take them to the perfect place, but something went wrong and he had to shoot them instead. The circle is complete."

"What do you mean complete?" Stammerwood said.

"I mean that I think the next body will turn up *in* the

park."

"Why?"

"He's already traced a circle around it for the last three years. He's now announced that he will be giving us a body today at midday. I think he's putting on a show."

"A show?" Stammerwood questioned.

"Yeah. Some kind of big display to prove how good he is at what he does. The only thing is I don't think he would have expected us to look at the shooting sites. This only came up because I thought about the night that he almost killed me."

"So you think you can find him?"

"Maybe, but I don't think we will get anywhere today. The body will turn up in the park, I'm certain of that. It may already be there for all we know, waiting to be found, or an anonymous tip may get called in at midday to say that it has been found. Either way, we know that after today he will have completed his puzzle."

"Then what happens?" Garroway asked.

"That's what I'm trying to understand."

"Understand this," Stammerwood said. "He has told us that everyday that we do not catch him a body will turn up on the street. That is a serious threat. We have no time for games. We need to catch this fucker, and now."

"That's understood, chief. But I think to him this is all a big game."

"What kind of game is running around the city killing innocent women?" Stammerwood's voice was now raised.

"The worst game for the sickest mind, but one that we are currently playing to try and catch him."

The room feel silent as the realisation of that last comment kicked in. The usual clacking on typewriters, and phones ringing, all seemed to stop. The clock on the wall seemed to be ticking extremely loud in the silence.

# NINE

The next twenty minutes flew by in what seemed like seconds. As soon as the clock ticked into the twelfth hour of the day, the phone on Harlow's desk rang.

"Chicago PD, Detective Harlow speaking?"

"Southeast side of Douglas Park detective. Better luck next time."

Harlow opened his mouth to reply but the line went dead. He slowly replaced the receiver and looked up.

"Southeast side of the park. Come on, Charlie."

"I'll get a unit down there right away," Stammerwood said. "Liaise with them when you arrive."

Harlow nodded as he grabbed his hat and coat from the stand and headed for the door.

---

The Mainline pulled up to the south entrance of Douglas Park. As both of the detectives got out onto the sidewalk, Harlow lit a cigarette and headed for the destination.

"You know those things will kill you one day right?" Garroway said, as he walked alongside.

"If they don't, then the job will," Harlow replied. "Besides, they soothe me. All the time they do that, I'll keep smoking them."

Garroway nodded at him to acknowledge the answer, despite not believing it. They entered the park and it wasn't long before the usual police presence became obvious. There were five officers over near a tree in the southeast corner; the yellow police tape had already been used to cordon off the area, stretching between three giant oaks. The other officers were standing around, talking with each other. As Harlow and Garroway approached the officer in front of the tape, he nodded once and let them past.

"No ID this time?" Garroway said.

"They know who we are," Harlow confirmed.

"Usually there are rules around this kind of thing."

"Maybe the chief is being a bit lenient at the moment. He knew we were coming, and wouldn't be far behind these guys. Maybe he called ahead. Who knows?"

As the detectives walked further into the crime scene a man came towards them. He was in his mid-thirties, his black hair was unkempt on his head, and his glasses balanced unevenly at the end of his nose. They recognised him: forensics detective, Dean Walton.

"Harlow. Garroway," he said, jittery, nodding at both of them.

"Walton," Harlow responded. "What have we got?"

"Well, let's just say he's upped his game for this one. Not the usual."

"How do you mean?" Harlow asked.

"Take a look for yourselves."

Harlow walked around the forensics officer, and was greeted by a sight that he wasn't expecting.

Before him was a blonde haired girl; naked and bound with her arms tied around the tree. As he walked around the body, he noticed that the index finger on her right hand was missing; the cut looked to have been a little rough, down to the knuckle.

*The finger that had been delivered.*

The purple marks that laced the neckline were also present. Her left hand clasped a single stemmed red rose, which tied the whole scene together.

"He's gone in a very different direction," Garroway said, as he appeared behind Harlow.

"Different is one way of looking at it. Usually he just leaves them on the street, nothing fancy, they are usually clothed too." Walton mused, as he approached from behind.

"So why has he done this?" Garroway directed the question towards Harlow.

"Beats me," he replied. "I thought he might want to put a show on with this one. I wasn't too far wrong but I wasn't expecting this either. Any sign of her clothes?"

"Not that we've come across yet," Walton said. "You sound like you were expecting this body?"

"I knew another one would appear, but I didn't think it would be in this vein," he said.

"I don't understand the finger," Walton said. "The previous bodies never had anything missing."

"Can you estimate the time of death?" Harlow asked, side-stepping the comment.

"Well from the initial looks of it, I would say twenty-four hours, maybe a little longer. The bruising is still clearly apparent around the neck, and the body hasn't lost too much colour."

"So she's not fresh then?" Harlow asked for confirmation.

"Definitely not," Walton said, pushing the glasses back up his nose.

Harlow nodded.

"You got any ideas?" Garroway asked.

"None yet," Harlow responded. "Can we either cut her down, or get her covered up. The last thing we need is her to attract anymore unwanted attention," Harlow asked loudly towards the crew working the scene.

A couple of the officers nodded and headed around to the other side of the tree, to where the girl was bound, and cut the restraints. There were two officers in front of the body to gather it as it went limp, and they placed her onto the ground.

"Be careful," Walton started, stammering at the men doing it. "Don't damage the body."

The men glanced knowingly at him. Dean Walton had a reputation for being a perfectionist. No matter what state the body was discovered in, he still treated it as though it was a delicate flower. Harlow turned from the scene, took a cigarette out of his pack and lit it. As he exhaled, a plume of smoke came out of his mouth, clouding the area before him. As he went to take another drag, Stammerwood appeared through the mist.

"Well? What have we got?"

"The girl was found naked, bound to a tree, missing her right index finger. The usual M.O. for cause of death, albeit slightly different in presentation, along with a single red rose in her left hand," Harlow answered.

"Naked? Why was she naked?" The chief asked.

"Beats me chief. They've not found the clothes yet, either."

"Dammit," he spat. "We need to find this guy, Harlow. I can't have bodies turning up like this around the city."

"I know, chief."

"You need to find out what his plan is and where he is hiding. I guess we have no idea who this poor girl is yet?"

"Not yet. We need to wait until the body reaches the morgue, and then run her prints through the system. Or find some ID for her."

An officer shouted from afar. "Found some clothes over here!"

There was a slight hubbub as people reacted to the call, with Garroway running over to grab the bag from the officer. He walked straight back to Harlow and the chief, and placed the black bin bag down on the ground before them. Harlow crouched down to the bag, but Walton prevented him from opening it with an outstretched hand.

He moved Harlow aside and, using his gloved hands, slowly opened the bag. He pulled the items of clothing out from within and laid them on the ground around himself. There were a pair of blue jeans, a white shirt, some white underwear, and a white bra.

*Simple taste,* Harlow thought, as he glanced over the clothes.

Walton then proceeded to inspect each item of clothing. The shirt and underwear were quick, and as expected had nothing on them. As he reached the jeans, he put his hand into one of the front pockets and pulled out a crumpled ten-dollar bill, and some change. The back pocket came with a neatly folded note.

Walton slowly unfolded it, and seeing what was on the page held it up for Harlow to take. As Harlow looked at the page, the words jumped out at him like a Jack in the Box.

*One more. Twenty-Four hours.*

. . .

"What the hell?" Stammerwood said.

"He's telling us that, in twenty-four hours, we will have another body," Harlow replied.

"He's got some bloody nerve. You've got twenty-four hours to find him. I can't have another body turning up."

Harlow sighed. "So you keep saying."

"Listen to me, *detective,* I think you need to understand the chain of command here. I tell you to do it and you do it. We don't do things your way. We tried that this morning, but now I have to tell the board that we keep receiving these notes. That means that you *need* to find this guy, and quickly. Do I make myself clear?"

"Extremely," Harlow responded.

He turned and walked away from the scene, leaving the chief and the officers behind him. Garroway followed him quickly, until he was alongside.

"Look, Ian. Stammerwood is just pissed because this is happening on his streets. Anyone would be the same. Don't take it too seriously."

"That's easy for you to say, Charlie. This guy is targeting me personally. He's calling me out and testing me, challenging me to find him. I wanna find this sonofabitch more than anything."

"I know, Ian, but whatever the chief says, don't take it personally."

"That prick can go to hell for all I care. I will find this guy. I just don't know if I can do it within the next twenty-four hours. It might be that another couple of bodies will show up before I catch him. By then, it might be my badge on the line. Hell, it might be yours too. I need to know you're okay with that, before we go any further."

"Hey, Ian. I'll be with you all the way. When have I ever let you down?"

"You're the one person that never has," Harlow said, smiling at him.

He patted him on the shoulder and headed towards the car.

"You okay to get a ride back to the station with someone else? I need to try and get some rest before hitting this hard again."

"Sure thing. But don't be too long, the chief will be after your ass."

"Tell him I'm chasing a lead if he asks. Tell him that's all I gave you. I'll only be an hour or two. Wanna clear my head, have a shower and get a change of clothes, and I'll be right as rain. Hopefully, with a pair of fresh eyes, I'll be able to do some good. In the meantime, look over those files in a bit more detail for me, will ya? It'll be good to have an idea of what we are looking for."

"Sure thing."

Harlow reached his car, opened the door and got in. He stared long and hard at the crime scene that was not too far ahead of him, placed his head on the steering wheel and closed his eyes. When he opened them and looked back out of the windscreen, he could see Garroway heading towards an incoming Stammerwood.

"Spin him a good tail for me, Charlie," Harlow said to himself.

# TEN

Harlow started the ignition and headed south before pulling onto West Cermark Road. He continued before turning north on Harlem Avenue, and then took a left onto West Roosevelt Road before arriving at Forest Home Cemetery.

When he killed the motor, he sat for a moment just staring out at the greenery before him. He exited the car and walked through the gates. He followed the path that he knew all too well, and arrived at the headstone.

> *Here lies Katherine Harlow*
> *1906 – 1946*
> *Forever loved and forever missed.*

Harlow crouched down and moved some of the rubbish from around the gravesite, and pulled up a couple of weeds.

"Hi, beautiful," he said. "I'm sorry I've not been around in a month or two, works been kinda hectic. I hope mum and dad are looking after you up there. I need your help, as always."

He sniffed back a tear as he spoke.

"I gotta find this guy, Katherine. Really, I have. If there's any kinda sign you can give me to help."

He stared upwards at the slowly greying sky above him for a while. He snorted slightly as he lowered his head back down to the grave. When he looked closer, he noticed there was something underneath the last bunch of flowers. He moved them and sitting there, atop the grave of his dead wife, was a fresh, single stemmed red rose.

"You sonofabitch," Harlow growled.

He picked up the rose and looked around the deserted cemetery. There was no one around, no people visiting any other sites, and no one doing any maintenance. Harlow was met with an eerie silence.

He held the rose in his hand, wondering if it was just his mind playing tricks.

*It could have been a relative paying their respects. No, don't be so stupid, it's obvious where it's come from.*

*But why?*

*Why would he come to my wife's grave and place a rose here? Another way to get at me? There's no way he could know that much about me, is there?*

He snapped himself back into reality, and looked at the head stone again.

"I'll find him, Kate. You know I will. No matter what it takes, I'll catch him. I pray you'll help me before it gets too late."

He looked up at the sky once more.

"I love you, baby. I miss you."

He kissed his upturned hand and placed it gently onto the top of the head stone, before turning and walking through the cemetery, back to his car. When he got in, he placed the rose on the passenger seat, stared at it for a long moment, and headed back on the road towards his apartment.

# ELEVEN

As he pulled up outside of his apartment, he sat with his head back on the seat and stared at the ceiling. He couldn't get over the nagging feeling that the killer had visited his wife's grave. The thought just kept playing repeatedly in his mind. There were things that the killer had done over the years, to many people that had never deserved it, but this was taking it to another level. Challenging him was one thing, but bringing it to his home was something completely different.

He opened the door and walked into his old, rundown apartment. Since his wife had died eight years ago, he had moved out of their family house and into the one bedroom abode. Because of commitments to work he was hardly ever there, so didn't care much for the state of it. He wandered through the living area and into the bedroom, before collapsing down onto the bed.

Four hours later, Harlow opened his eyes and strained to focus. He looked down at his watch, saw the time, and cursed. He jumped up, grabbed a clean suit off the rail and quickly changed. He ran into the bathroom, brushed his teeth, and smoothed his hair down. As he grabbed his hat and coat and headed for the door, the phone rang. Harlow picked it up on the third ring.

"Hello?"

"Harlow, where the hell have you been?" The voice bellowed through the receiver at him, loud and clear.

"Chief?" Harlow asked, still slightly dazed.

"It's Stammerwood. Where have you been? Garroway said you needed to chase some leads and would only be an hour. That was over four hours ago."

"I know, chief. I had a couple of things to follow up, and asked Charlie to go through the files in my absence. Is everything alright?"

"You mean other than the shit storm we've got going on down here because of the body found in the park earlier today?"

"That's what I meant."

"Well, the commissioner has been made aware that we have received threats about other bodies turning up. He wants to take it higher but I have convinced him to give us a bit of time. I need to know that you can catch this guy."

Harlow paused for a beat.

"Harlow? You still there?"

"Yeah, chief. Sorry I was thinking."

"Well? Can you catch him?"

"I think I can, chief."

"What makes you so confident?"

"He's gotta slip up sooner or later. When he does, I'll be ready."

"You can't let all of this hang on him making a mistake! What if he doesn't? Plus, how many more women will have to die before that happens?"

"Chief, calm down. I'm on my way into the station now. When I get there, I'll have a chat with Charlie and see what he's managed to dig up by going through the cases. When we've caught up, I'll come and see you and inform you of our plan."

"You're that confident that you'll have a plan after you've spoken to him?"

"I have a gut feeling."

"A gut feeling is not a plan, detective."

"I know that, chief, but I also know what this guy's motive is."

Harlow put the receiver back down whilst Stammerwood was still talking. He could hear the muffled words all the way, until he clicked it on the holder.

He lit a cigarette and headed outside. The rain had started to fall now, the drops hitting him like mini, ice-cold bullets. He was sure that snow was due, but had to deal with the rain and biting cold until it happened.

*At least it didn't rain this afternoon*, he thought, as he headed down the steps of his apartment building, and climbed into his car. He slammed the door shut and put the radio on as he started to drive; a jazz melody filled the air, instantly calming him. He'd always liked to listen to the jazz numbers when he drove; it cleared his head.

As he pulled up outside the station, Garroway stepped off the sidewalk. He opened the door as an umbrella was placed over him, to keep the detective dry.

"Charlie," Harlow nodded.

"Ian," Garroway responded.

"Why the five star treatment? A bit of rain never hurt anyone."

"We need to talk."

"About what?"

"The files, Ian. I've ripped through each and every one of them. I've got nothing. *We've* got nothing."

"I'm sure there's something in them."

"I'm telling you, Ian. There's nothing that we don't already know."

"We didn't know about the victims turning up on a two block radius until we went through the shooting files. There's gotta be something."

"Stammerwood tells me that once we've talked, you're going to see him with a plan. Well I hate to break it to you, but it seems pretty thin on the ground."

"First things first. I need a coffee. After that, tell me what you've found out from the files. Once we've gone through that, I'll lay my plan on you."

"You're that confident?"

"You have to be sometimes, Charlie. I'm … we're not gonna catch him by sitting on our asses and doing nothing. He's got to have made a mistake somewhere along the line. Come on, let's get out of this weather."

The two detectives crowded under the small umbrella and headed into the warmth of the station.

As Harlow walked into the precinct, Stammerwood confronted him. He tried avoiding him, but the chief matched his movements.

"Well?" Stammerwood asked.

"Jeez, chief. Can I get into the precinct first before you pounce on me? I told you I need to discuss the findings with Charlie, and then we'll come and speak to you. Give me an hour."

"An hour? You have thirty minutes. I need some answers, and I need them now."

Harlow nodded and pushed his way past Stammerwood. He made it over to the coffee pot at the back of the room, and poured himself a cup of the black liquid. His desk was piled high with paperwork when he reached it. He moved a couple aside, placed his coffee down, sat in the chair, and lit up a cigarette. Charlie sat in the seat opposite him with a coffee of his own, and began to talk.

"So, as I said, I got nothing. I went through all of the files and have come up with no new ideas, or theories, or anything whilst you've not been here."

"Right. Were you able to tie anything into the shooting files?"

"Other than we think it was done by the same person, no."

"Okay. Well, that we already knew. I want you to get me a list of every gun vendor in the area. Find out which stores stock Berettas, and which ones keep records. If we go back to just before all of this started, then maybe we will be able to narrow it down a little."

"You think he'd have gotten the piece just before the first killing?"

"At this moment I'm giving everything a go. My thought is he would've got the stuff just before he decided to start doing all of this. Been prepared. He knew that he'd need a gun as a backup, just in case any of the victims didn't go quietly."

"Okay," Garroway said, scribbling in his notebook.

"Do we know who the girl is yet?"

"Yeah, she's uh..." Garroway flicked through a couple of pages of his notepad. "Jessica Chambers. She was twenty-nine years old, lived out on Rosewood. She was reported missing five days ago."

"You get that info from missing persons?"

"Yeah. They had a picture up there from the parents. Put it next to the corpse and bingo, we had a match."

"How many other woman were reported missing in the last few days, matching our usual description?"

"Six."

Garroway opened a file, fanned out six pictures of various sizes, and turned them towards Harlow. He sat forward in his chair and moved closer to see them properly.

"We got names for all these, with addresses?"

"Each and every one of them."

"Okay. I want you to send some officers to each of the houses. Get me any information that you can about them, where they worked, friends, anything at all. I wanna know as much about these girls as possible. Chances are he has them all already, and is just deciding which one to give us and when."

"You think they're dead already?"

"No. I think he will kill these girls on the day of the drop. The one in the park today was unusual, and different for him. I think he did it in an attempt to throw us off the scent. Now, I think he will go back to his usual ways."

Harlow sat staring at the girls' pictures. Each of them were attractive, looked to be around the same age, and had all gone missing in the last few days. These girls had to be next, which meant that the killer would need to store them somewhere. A house big enough to store six or more people was not the easiest to come by in the city. And he knew that having them all next to each other in a room would get them talking. The killer wasn't into hurting them as none of the previous bodies showed any signs of abuse or injuries before they were murdered. It had to be somewhere that he could keep them separate from each other.

"Charlie," Harlow said, snapping out of his thoughts. "Did any of the autopsies for the girls show any signs of drugs in their bodies?"

Garroway flicked through the notes that he had made on the files.

"Not all of them, but a few of them had a high dosage of sleeping pills in their system."

"That'll be how he's keeping them quiet and not hurting them. He's drugging them with high doses, but not high enough to do them any damage or risk their life. He's then taking them to his chosen location and strangling them."

"Who would know to do that?"

"That's the question that we need to answer. First, we need to report our findings to the chief. Go and get some officers, send them to these girl's houses, and meet me in there in a few minutes."

"Sure thing."

Garroway stood up and headed across the room. Harlow took a long drag on his cigarette before extinguishing the butt in an over flowing ashtray. He then headed across the precinct, and into the chiefs office.

# TWELVE

"So?" Stammerwood asked, without even looking up from his paperwork.

"We've got a couple of things to go on, chief." Harlow said.

"You going to tell me or just stand there?"

"Well, we feel that he's keeping the women in a secure location. There have been six women taken in the last few days that all fit the correct profile of his usual victim. By going back through the files, we have also found that there were large traces of sleeping pills in a few of the girl's blood streams. We think that this is how he is keeping them quiet and why they're not trying to get away before he kills them and deposits the body."

Stammerwood sat nodding for a moment whilst staring through the blinds, his focus on something outside of the window.

"What are you doing about it?" he asked.

"Charlie is currently sending some uniforms to the homes of the girls that have gone missing. They are gonna get as much information as they can on them to see if we can find out where they were taken from."

"Okay. And what about the sleeping pill thing? The guy's got to be an expert right? A chemist or something? Giving them enough tablets to knock them out, but not have them overdose, is a tricky skill."

"That's my thinking too. I'm gonna check where the girls were registered, see if there is any common ground there. Might be a doctor or someone with a background in medicine. Either way; a large amount of sleeping pills is not something that one can easily come by."

"Fine. Do what you need to do. At least I can go to the board with something. Just remember that the commissioner will want someone to take the fall for this if we can't catch this guy. I'm telling you now, it won't be me."

Harlow bowed his head slightly, turned, and walked back out of the office. As he approached his desk, Garroway appeared.

"All good?" Harlow asked him.

"As good as it can be. Got three sets of uniforms heading out to the girls' houses now. In addition, I got another one of them going through the files to see if he can find out who their doctors were. Thought I'd get a head start on that instead of interrupting your talk with the chief. How'd that go?"

"Fine. He has something that he can give to the big wigs so he's happy. I want us to work on this big house theory. He's gotta be keeping them somewhere, within easy access of where he picks them up, and easy access for dropping them off. Move these, will ya?"

The detectives moved the remainder of the paperwork from the desk, until only the map remained.

"Okay. From what we worked out yesterday, this is his field of play."

Harlow moved his hand in a circular motion, following the circles and crosses of the marked locations, where the bodies were discovered.

"It needs to be somewhere fairly near to here, or somewhere that's quick and easy to get in and out of," he continued.

"Well, it's not going to be in the circle," Garroway said.

"And whys that?"

"I don't think he'd kill and take the bodies outwards in a circle from his house It would almost be like a big target. It's one of the first places we would go."

"Fair point. In which case, we are moving slightly away. My guess is he keeps an eye on the streets. He doesn't want foot patrols to see him. He would have picked the girls up and driven them somewhere."

"What about here?" Garroway said, whilst pointing at the map.

"Maybe. I don't see it myself, but it's worth a try. I think he'd go more towards the lake. You can get some big units out there, warehouses even, buildings that aren't used. Perfect place to hide a load of people. Plus, if he had a truck, no one would think twice about seeing one drive in and out of a warehouse."

"I think you're on to something there. The only problem is there are a lot of warehouses covering a lot of ground."

"Yeah, you're right, Charlie."

Harlow stretched back in his chair and craned his neck upwards.

"Where did you go earlier, Ian?" Garroway suddenly asked.

"I went home. I needed some rest. I'd been at this place for thirteen hours before stopping. That okay with you?"

"Yeah, of course. Just unlike you to take off in the middle of an investigation."

"I didn't take off. As I said, I went home to get some rest. I needed to look at this thing with some fresh eyes."

"Good idea, I guess."

"It helped me see these things so I'll say it was worthwhile. Anyway, I ended up taking longer than I thought. As soon as my head hit the pillow, I was out for the count. Surprised I could sleep at all, to be honest."

"We both know that you love the chase, Ian."

Harlow let a slight smile creep across his face. It was true; he always loved the chase, loved getting near and eventually catching the criminals. The only problem with this one: it had gone on for so long, and completely drained him. He pulled himself out of his thoughts and back to the grey precinct room that surrounded him.

"Come on. Let's get out of this place and go for a drive. I think we should go and have a look at some potential locations for our killer."

"Sounds good to me."

## THIRTEEN

As the Mainline headed out from the parking lot and headed east towards the lake, the clouds started to gather overhead and the temperature dropped. Harlow cranked the heat up in the car.

"Damn, its cold at the moment," Garroway commented, whilst rubbing his hands together and then holding them close to his mouth, blowing on them.

"Yeah, you're tellin' me," Harlow answered.

"You think we're going to find anything out there?"

"We'll know soon enough. We just need to get an idea, see if there is anything we can discover at these places. There might be an abandoned warehouse or something that we can see. Either way we need to look. I'm starting to think the chief believes that we don't wanna catch this guy."

"You're not getting out of the station just for the sake of getting out of there, are you?"

Harlow took a cigarette out of his pack and lit it, inhaling the smoke deeply into his lungs before blowing it out again.

"You are, aren't you?" Garroway pushed.

"No. I need to get out of there. I feel like I've been

cooped up in that place for the last few days. Besides, the chief is breathing down my neck and driving me crazy. But that's not why we are heading out here. We're coming out here because I think there is a chance that we might actually be able to catch this guy."

"Hmm. Well, as long as there is a point to this little adventure, then that's fine."

"Don't start trying to tell me how things are gonna go. Have I ever led you wrong before?"

"No, but there's a first time for everything."

Harlow ignored the last comment and stared out of the windscreen, watching the road as they continued onwards towards their destination.

The city blocks before them started to fall away the further out they drove. The traffic became sparse, the cars eventually replaced by trucks with various cargo, either coming from or going to the lakes.

"One day this place will be booming. You know that?" Harlow said.

"Yeah maybe. They seem to love it up here."

Harlow nodded as he drove.

As they arrived at the waterfront, there were countless workers in the area; all helping each other carry materials or moving various crates.

"Ian, he wouldn't be here. It's too crowded," Garroway said.

"Yeah I agree. Let's move up slightly."

Turning north, they slowly started to drive up the lakeside, seeing all of the different warehouses as they went. Most of them were full and had people outside of them completing various tasks. The others that remained empty were being used as car parks for the employees and other warehouses, or had kids running wild within them.

"This is a waste of time. Maybe you were wrong on this one," Garroway said.

Harlow ignored him and continued to crawl up the road, staring at each warehouse as he went. He didn't want to give up that easily, didn't want this endeavour to produce a dead end.

"Come on, Ian. You know I'm right on this one. Lets head back and see if there's anything else that's come up, or head over to the morgue to have a look at the new body. They might have something for us."

"No."

The words hung in the air for a moment, and neither of the men spoke for a while. Harlow then noticed two warehouses side by side that were unused. There were no cars parked out front, and no kids in the area.

He slowed and pulled in before the building. The tires crunched over the gravel as the car turned off the road. He ground to a stop and shut off the engine.

Garroway looked across at him.

"We going in there?"

Harlow nodded.

"Grab the flash lights will ya? We'll do a quick sweep of these two. If neither of them provide any clues, then we'll head back. Maybe go to the morgue as you suggested. Deal?"

"Yeah, that sounds fair."

The two detectives got out of the car and stood in the dim light for a moment. The rain had stopped for now, but the air was bitingly cold.

Harlow looked around the area, noticing that there was nothing near by. No workmen, no kids, no movement, no nothing. Considering that, just down the road, all of the other warehouses were alive with people, it seemed odd to him that this area was silent.

He took one final drag on his cigarette before dropping it onto the floor and stubbing it out with his shoe. He flicked the flashlight on. Garroway did the same.

As they approached the first rusted door, Harlow noticed the lack of a padlock. He unclipped his holster and pulled his Colt out from under his jacket, holding it up in his right hand. He passed his flashlight to Garroway to hold whilst he yanked on the handle and pulled the rusting metal door open.

It screeched under the strain of being moved for the first time in ages, and wheeled across to the right. The stale fish smell hit them full in the face and both men turned their heads away to try and catch some fresh air. Garroway handed him back the flashlight and Harlow held it out in front of him with his left hand, as he stepped into the darkness.

The light pierced the black warehouse with its small beam. Harlow stepped inside and veered left, swiftly followed by Garroway who went right. Harlow had his gun raised and traced the beam of the flashlight with it.

"Clear this way," Garroway announced.

"Yeah, same over here," Harlow replied.

Harlow kept his gun up and walked slowly through the warehouse. The debris on the floor was cracking and sloshing as he stepped. When he reached the wall there was a loud click, and then the darkness around him started to become clearer. As Harlow looked across the other side of the vast space he saw Garroway stood at a large switch, looking in his direction. Harlow squinted slightly as he looked up into the bulbs hanging from the ceiling, which were growing in brightness. Within thirty seconds the whole place was fully illuminated. They could see into each of the corners, and to the far end.

All of it was the same, just empty space. The floor

beneath him was covered in trash from when the previous people had vacated the premises some time before.

Garroway walked over and joined Harlow in the centre of the space, clicking off his flashlight as he reached him.

"This one's a bust then," he said.

"Yeah, so it seems," Harlow replied.

"Let's check the next one."

Harlow nodded and turned for the door. Garroway wandered off, doused the lights before exiting, and closed the huge door behind them.

As the detectives started to head towards the next warehouse, they could hear the crackle of their radio coming from the car.

"I'll grab it," Harlow said. "Carry on and I'll catch up."

Garroway headed off towards the second warehouse as Harlow rounded towards the car. As he reached it and pulled the door open he heard the radio call.

"Harlow. Harlow, come in. Harlow, are you there?"

Harlow reached across and grabbed the receiver, pushed down on the button on the side and spoke.

"This is Harlow."

"Thank God you're there. We've had another body."

Harlow lowered his head. "Chief, that you?"

"Yeah, it's me. What difference does that make? Did you hear what I said?"

"Yeah, I did. Sorry. It was a surprise to hear you on the radio was all. Where is it?"

"Englewood and 53rd. I've got a couple of officers on their way now but I want you out there."

"Is it our guy again?"

"From what we know. The call came in five minutes ago from a woman that came across the body. You with Garroway?"

"Yeah, we're down at the docks by the lakes, looking at warehouses."

"Well, get your ass down there now. We need to know what's going on with this."

"We're on it, chief."

Harlow hooked the CB back onto the holder and leaned back out of the car.

"*Garroway!*" He shouted.

His partner had just reached the entrance to the warehouse and was going to open the door when he heard the call. When he looked over, Harlow gestured for him to come over and join him. His partner jogged over towards the car, his coat flapping behind him like a cape.

"What's up?" he said, a little short of breath.

"We've got another body. Chief just called it in, wants us over there now."

"*Another* body?" He asked.

"Yeah."

"Is it another one from our guy?"

"Apparently so. Called in a few minutes ago by a woman that found it. Come on. We'll come back here another time."

Garroway opened the passenger door and got in alongside Harlow. They pulled round and back out onto the road.

"Why is there another body?" Garroway asked. "Didn't he say twenty-four hours to you on the phone?"

"Yeah. He's early."

"Why's he early? It isn't his style."

"Beats me. If there's another body though, we need to go look at it."

## FOURTEEN

As the car came to a stop at the curb, a police car opposite them sat idle, its lights flashing. Two officers were pulling yellow crime scene tape across an alleyway, and there was another officer turning away any unwanted visitors as they tried to take a peek.

The detectives headed over to the scene, flashed their badges, and ducked under the tape, entering the alley. As they walked down the alley, they came face to face with Dean Walton.

"You guys made good time," he said as a greeting.

"We weren't too far away. What's the situation?" Harlow replied.

"Pretty standard scene for our guy, this one. I wont bore you with the obvious details of the victim. Unlike the park this one is fully clothed, and pretty much the same as all the other ones we've seen."

Harlow nodded and stepped round Walton to where the body lay on the floor. He bent down and tilted his head slightly to look at the girl's face.

There was no expression on it at all; just a calm lifeless

gaze looked up at him. He reached down and lightly closed her eyes with the tips of his fingers.

"Detective!" Walton said angrily from behind him. "Don't tamper with the body. You know better than to contaminate the scene."

"I was closing her eyes. That such a crime?"

Realising the situation, he thought that was probably not the best choice of words, but it was too late now.

"You never touch the body. You *know* that."

"Okay, I'm sorry. I just thought she deserved to be at peace is all."

"Well, let us do that next time."

"Fine."

Harlow stood up, pulled a cigarette from his pack and lit it, filling his lungs with the smoke that he craved, before exhaling it into the night sky. He looked down at the body once more, noticing the purple marks round her neck, and then the default rose in her left hand.

"How do you explain the decision to put on an elaborate display in the park, and then go back to basics for this one?" Harlow asked Walton.

"Beats me," he said, not looking up from the body.

"Why make such a show of the last body, but not this one. I don't get it."

"As I said, it beats me."

"I wasn't asking … don't worry. I'm guessing it's the usual cause of death?"

"Yep. Strangled the life out of her. Must be a horrible way to go," he said whilst staring at her face.

"Yeah, it must be." Harlow agreed.

"Excuse me? Detective Harlow?"

An officer had appeared just behind the small group. They spun around to face him.

Harlow nodded. "Yeah?"

"Chief Stammerwood is on the radio for you. Says it's important."

He rolled his eyes towards Garroway.

"Fine. Where abouts?"

"Just over at the car."

Harlow looked at Garroway. "Stick around here and see what you can get from the scene. Maybe have a wander around and see if anything sticks out as unusual."

"It's not my first time, don't worry about me. See what Stammerwood wants you for this time."

Harlow followed the officer to his car, who reached in through the window and pulled out a radio receiver. He handed it to Harlow.

"This is Harlow."

"We've got another fucking body."

The answer stunned Harlow, and caused him to stand there frozen for a beat.

"Harlow? Did you hear me?"

The words came out of the radio loud and angry.

"Yeah, chief. Sorry, did you say we've got *another* body?"

"Yes I did. The corner of East 23rd Street."

"Call just come in?"

"A few minutes ago. What difference does that make?"

"None, I just wanted to know if it was a recent thing is all. Same as this? As in by our guy?"

"From what the person said that called it in, yeah."

Harlow hit the side of the door with an open hand.

*What was this guy up to? He'd never done this before. He told me twenty-four hours. And that should have only been another body at most, not two in the space of half an hour.*

"Okay, chief. We'll head over there."

"Make sure you do. Somehow I've gotta keep the press off of this. They catch wind and it'll be all over the front page of the Tribune in the morning."

Harlow chucked the receiver back into the car and walked back down the alleyway, to where Garroway was chatting with Walton.

"Everything all right?"

"We've got another body," he said slowly.

"You're shitting me?" Garroway asked.

"I wish I was. We've gotta go."

"I'll see you there," Walton said to the two of them. "Got to finish this one first before I can start on another."

"Yeah sure," Harlow answered over his shoulder, as they walked towards the car.

They opened the doors and got in.

"What is this guy playing at?" Garroway asked.

"I've been asking myself the same question. Whatever it is, it's not good."

"What's your gut feeling telling you now?"

"That I wanna catch this guy more than anything else," he said, as he fired up the Mainline and pulled back out onto the road, heading for the next crime scene.

## FIFTEEN

As they pulled up to the curb and went to step out, the radio crackled once more.

"Harlow. Harlow come in," the dejected voice said.

"This is Harlow," he said, grabbing the radio out of the handle.

"We have another body."

"Another one? We've just got to the second one, chief."

"No, it's another one. Hang on." The line went dead for a moment.

"What the hell does he mean we got *another* body? Surely he's getting his wires crossed?" Garroway said.

"We will find out soon enough, I'm sure."

The radio crackled to life. "Better make that three more bodies. Two more have just been called in."

"So there's another three bodies on top of the one we've just come from, and the one we are at now?" Harlow asked.

"That's right."

"Chief, we can't get round all of them at the same time."

"I know. Focus yourself on where you are now. I'll have

to get the other bodies into the morgue and you'll have to go and look at them there."

Harlow sat for a moment counting in his head.

"Chief?" he said.

"Yeah?"

"I don't mean to be the bearer of bad news, but the reports we got from the missing persons desk indicated six females were reported missing that matched the usual description of his victims. With the three you've just been informed of, and the two we have already gone to tonight, that makes five. I think there will be another one."

The line went silent. Harlow imagined Stammerwood sat at his desk with his mouth open, the cogs in his brain turning as he tried to connect the dots, to comprehend the information he just received.

"Fuck," Stammerwood said, slowly and concisely.

"Yeah I echo that one, chief. If the other one comes through, have it taken to the morgue with the rest. When the guys go out to the crime scenes have them take lots of pictures. We will get to as many of the scenes as we can and see if anything sticks out. My guess is that there won't be much. He doesn't like to leave clues."

"The only thing he likes to leave are dead bodies and a trail of fucking roses," the chief said, the anger clear in his voice. "You need to find this fucker, and it needs to be *now*. Do I make myself clear?"

"You always do, chief."

"None of your games. He needs to be caught. We're gonna have the entire department come down on our ass for this."

"I know, chief. We'll do what we can here. Send some other guys to the other areas. Make sure that they know what they're doing though. I don't want a couple of average Joes kicking through the scene and making more of a mess. I know some of the guys we have down there."

"Don't start telling me what to do, *detective*. Do your jobs, but do it better and do it now."

Harlow put the radio back into the holder and smashed his hand on the steering wheel.

"What the *fuck*?" Garroway said. "What is this guy doing?"

"He's playing us is what he's doing, taking us for fools, and rubbing our noses in it."

"How is he getting rid of the bodies at this speed?"

"I don't know."

Harlow snatched the radio up again and pressed the button.

"Chief?"

"Yeah?" The voice answered.

"The calls that came in for these bodies. Were they all done by women?"

"What?"

"Were they all called in by a woman?"

"The first three were. Hang on."

Harlow heard some commotion as Stammerwood called out to someone in the station. He'd forgotten to take his finger fully off the button. The muted voices came across the airwaves as he asked to find out who took the other calls, and to find out if the callers were women. A minute later he came back on properly.

"Harlow?"

"I'm here, chief."

"Yeah, all of the calls were made by a woman. I don't see what…"

"Did you take any of the calls?" Harlow interrupted.

"The second two, yeah. Why?"

"Did the voice sound the same to you?"

"What?"

"Did it sound like it could have been the same person?"

"I'm not overly sure. It was a woman. Sounded hysterical each time. There's a lot of noise here too."

"Think about it, chief."

There was silence again for thirty seconds.

"Maybe, I guess. It would be hard to say for sure."

"What if there is someone helping him? An accomplice? He could be depositing the bodies, then, however long later, a woman phones the station in a state, declaring she's found the body."

"What makes you say that?"

"The only people we see when we get to these scenes are generally the people that are walking by and notice that something's going on. After a while, we see the press. You don't often see women on their own. Especially at night, and especially when these killings are coming to light again at the moment. What if someone is working with him?"

The thought hung the air for a while like a bad smell, until Stammerwood spoke again.

"When the next call comes through I'll try and take it. See if it sounds the same as the others did to me. Whatever is happening you need to go and look at the body. Find something to give me, and for us to go on."

"Will do, chief."

Harlow grabbed his hat off the back seat and placed it on top his head as he exited the car. As he walked towards the crime scene tape, he saw a guy coming towards him with a pen and paper in his hand.

"Detective Harlow. I'm Stan Mark…"

"I know who you are," Harlow said, cutting him off.

"…son of the Chicago Tribune," the man continued like it

had never happened. "Care to comment on the two murders that have happened tonight?"

"No," Harlow said, still walking.

The man was keeping pace alongside him.

"Is it true that these are more of The Rose Killer's victims?"

Harlow said nothing.

"What are you doing to catch him?"

Harlow said nothing.

"Are the department any closer to finding out who it is?"

Harlow said nothing.

"When are…"

"Stay right there, sir," one of the officers said, stepping in between him and Harlow. The detective stepped underneath the tape and out of reach.

"I just have a couple more questions."

Harlow heard the raised voice from over his shoulder. He didn't turn back, just carried on towards his destination.

"Fucking reporters," Garroway said.

"That's the guy that has done all of the digging. I had the pleasure of him come visit me in the hospital after my run in with the killer. Asks any question that will sell a story."

"Yeah, they all do," Garroway agreed.

"That piece of shit caused me no end of issues, I know that much. Always sticking his nose in where it's not wanted, and asking questions."

"I wouldn't want their job."

"Not many people would want ours," Harlow countered.

"True."

As they reached the body, it was almost like a mirror image of the previous two. "You take a look at the body. I'm gonna have a look around. See if there is anything that I can get from the area."

Garroway nodded, walked over and knelt down next to it. Harlow took a deep breath of the cold night air. It could rain, or maybe snow, if it stayed as cold as it had been recently. Either way, the weather would get shitty real soon.

He pulled a cigarette out, lit it, and took a walk around the alleyway. He saw one of the officers and asked him for his flashlight. With it in hand, he turned away and headed in the other direction, the light dancing off any object that was caught in its beam.

He scanned the dull, dirty walls. The trashcans were full and in need of emptying. He continued until he reached the end of the alley, and an opening to another street. At the end of the alleyway there were two more officers stood in front of the yellow tape facing away from him. In the distance behind them was a dark coloured car. It looked like a Buick but Harlow couldn't quite see it in the dull light. As he reached the officers and one of them turned, the cars lights came on. It pulled out onto the road and turned the corner away from the area.

"Hey. You guys notice that car?" Harlow asked, pointing.

The two detectives looked at each other.

"What car?" one of them replied.

"The one on the other side of the road, the one that just pulled away."

One of the men shook his head.

"Nah, sorry. We've just been standing here, stopping anyone from getting in," the other said.

"Fair enough."

Harlow glanced out on to the street but saw nothing that interested him or anything that seemed out of place. The car had bugged him but he didn't know why. He shook the thought out of his mind, turned, and headed back the way he had come, spraying the small light back across the dirty floor.

As he got back to the central part of the alleyway Garroway came strolling up to him.

"Nothing unusual here. Same as all the rest. You get anything?"

"No. There was a … never mind," Harlow said.

"There was a what?"

"It doesn't matter. Walton here yet?"

"No, we got someone else. Walton's been sent to one of the other crime scenes."

"Who is it?"

"Not sure. I've never met him before."

"Fair enough. Does he have any idea when she was killed?"

"He thinks she's pretty fresh. The last couple of hours by his estimates."

"So he's not pre-planning anymore then. This is happening as live as it can be."

"What do you mean?"

"The park was an elaborate display. He built up to it all with the finger and the notes. He called to say twenty-four hours, meaning, as far as I can see it, that it was gonna be another twenty-four hours until we had another body."

"That's what I thought too," Garroway chimed in.

"Exactly, but he's done it differently. Now there have been five bodies that we know of…"

"Six," Garroway interrupted. "You were right. One of the guys came up and told me not long after you headed down the alley."

"Fuck. I didn't wanna be right. In which case we have six bodies that have shown up on the street in the space of an hour. That's put his grand total up to twenty-five, but having eight bodies in the last three days makes me wonder how many more could be coming, that we *aren't* aware of."

"I've asked the missing person guys to let us know if any more women get reported missing with the same description as the vics. I checked in with them earlier and they hadn't had anymore, so we might be in the clear for a while."

"Don't be stupid. There's no way we're in the clear. He's sending us a message. A big 'fuck you, you can't catch me' message at that."

"We will get him, Ian."

"You're more confident than me right now. We've got nothing."

"You'll land on your feet. You always do. We all know that," Garroway said with a reassuring smile.

"Thanks. But the chief's patience is wearing thin. We need to nail this guy and quickly. The papers are all over this again, despite trying to keep it away from them."

"They will latch onto anything, you know that. They get a sniff that The Rose Killer is back in town and they'll run it until the ink runs out."

"That's the problem. We know the killer loves the attention, so if the papers start running their shit again, we may end up with more victims. It's only because his stories disappeared off the front pages that he stopped for a while."

"You don't know that, Ian."

"Hmm. It might as well be. It's what it seemed like, anyway."

"Look, you'll get him. I know you will. If he doesn't slip up then you'll just catch him some other way. Don't lose faith in yourself."

"Thanks, Charlie. I can always count on you to spin a brighter side to the tales."

Harlow patted Garroway on the shoulder as he headed past him and over to the forensics guy.

"Hey. I'm detective…"

"Harlow," the man cut in, pulling the mask down from his face.

"Hey, Tommy. Sorry, I didn't recognise you with the mask on. How've you been? I've not seen you in a while."

"I've been okay. Been working out of the area for a while. With all these bodies coming up thick and fast, Dean gave me a call to come down and help out."

"I'm gonna ask what we've got but I think I know the answer."

"Victim is Victoria Spencer. Twenty-seven years old. Lives only a few blocks from here. She was strangled to death. That part, I'm guessing you already knew."

"I guessed that much. Pretty standard with his victims. Didn't know who she was though. She gonna be taken to the morgue with the rest?"

"Yeah, she'll be taken soon. Just waiting on the coroners to get here and she'll be carted away. They're earning their money tonight, I know that much." He chuckled to himself.

"Sure are," Harlow agreed.

As he finished talking, there was a grumble of a van as it stopped at the entrance to the alleyway.

"Speaking of the coroners," Tommy said. "I've gotta sign the body over to them and head on to the next one. I'll see you soon, Ian."

"Yeah, see ya, Tommy. Take care of yourself."

Tommy nodded once and headed over to meet the advancing men that were dressed in black. One of them had turned away from Harlow, and the detective could see the word coroners written on the back of his jacket in white lettering. Harlow dropped his cigarette on the floor and stubbed it out with his shoe. He looked down at the girl's body on the floor and shook his head.

"I'll find him," he said under his breath.

"You talking to me?" Garroway said, approaching from behind.

"No. Just talking to myself. You ready?"

"Where we going now? Off to another body?"

"No, we'll head to the morgue. The first two bodies will be there by now. We can talk to the coroners when we get there and see if there is anything unusual about these bodies. I doubt there will be. It'll just be the usual shit."

"What about the other scenes?"

"I've told the chief to send people out there to take pictures of the areas. If I'm honest, I think it'll be similar to here and the others. We need to find something to try and make him slip up. If we can, we'll catch this sonofabitch."

"Agreed," Garroway said.

The two detectives walked back towards their car, through the growing throng of people that seemed to be gathering on the scene. As Harlow ducked under the tape, he was met by Stan Markson again.

"Detective Harlow. Can you tell me about the crime? Who was the girl?"

Harlow said nothing.

"Was she another victim of the Rose Killer?"

"Who said it was a girl?" Garroway said, spitefully towards the reporter.

The man stopped in his tracks looking slightly perplexed.

As they got into the car, Harlow said, "You shouldn't have said anything to him. They'll twist your words."

"I know, but it was fun to see him looking so confused," Garroway replied, as a smile crept across his face.

Harlow smirked, started the car, and headed towards the morgue.

## SIXTEEN

As the two men walked through the dull grey corridors of the morgue and opened the doors, they were hit with the strong smell of disinfectant.

There were four bodies lying atop the silver autopsy tables; all of them were covered in a sheet up to their necks. Donnie Jackson was standing over one of the bodies, shining a torch into the lifeless eyes of the body on the table.

"Donnie," Harlow said, approaching the man.

"Detective Harlow," he replied.

Donnie was a heavyset man with a balding pate. He was always sweaty, no matter the weather. Many people thought that's why he preferred working in the morgue, as it was cooler. He occasionally went out on to the streets to have an initial look at the victims, if work was slower. He liked to see them *fresh*, it was almost like a sick fetish he had. Despite that, he was the best at what he did.

"How are they looking? Anything new?" Harlow asked.

"Nothing that you don't probably already know," Donnie said without looking up.

"Is there anything that you can tell us?"

Donnie looked up at the detectives before stepping back. He grabbed a clipboard off the side and wrote something onto the paper attached to it.

"Detectives," he said, exhaling. "As you can see I'm in for a busy night here. You were at the scenes, you know the cause of death for these girls, so why are you asking?"

"Because this guy has given us six bodies in one night. The pressure is on my ass to deliver him to the chief. Now, I know you and I have never really seen eye to eye, but I need you to help me out here."

Donnie looked Harlow in the eye and nodded slowly.

"Fine. There is nothing out of the ordinary, detective. They were strangled to death, these two within the last two hours. The one over there, maybe about an hour ago. That's my best guess anyway."

"Have you run any tests yet?"

"What kind of tests would you like me to have done, detective? When I start on one body another gets wheeled in here. They'll take hours to process," he said whilst gesturing around.

"I wanna know if there were any drugs in their system. Or if there was a higher drug content than usual, in any of them?"

"We won't know that for another day or two I'm afraid, detective. The tests will get done but then they'll be sent off for analysis. I can put a rush on them for you, but I can't guarantee when it will be."

"Fine. If there's a rush put on it, can you let me know as soon as you get the results through?"

"Sure thing, detective. I'll make a note to send them right over to you. I'll probably wait until I have all of the bodies and send them over to be tested at the same time. It will make life a little easier."

"That'll be great. Thanks, Donnie."

"Don't mention it."

The two detectives turned and started to walk out. Before they reached the door, Donnie beckoned them once more. "Oh, and detective."

"Yeah?" he said, turning back.

"I know you've got to catch this guy but make sure they send someone else along soon. It's been a while since I've had this many bodies to examine." Donnie had a wry smile on his face and chuckled to himself as he turned towards the second body.

Harlow said nothing and pushed his way back through the door, down the corridor and out onto the street. As he reached his car, he noticed a dark car parked almost a block up on the other side of the road. He stood and stared for a second, it looked similar to the one he had seen earlier. The lights came on and the car pulled away from the curb and off into the night.

"You okay, Ian?" Garroway asked.

"What? Yeah I'm fine," Harlow responded.

"You don't seem with it."

"No, I'm okay. Sorry, I thought I saw something. Let's head back to the station. We'll have a chat with the chief and see if anything else has cropped up. The only plus is that no other bodies have been called in."

Harlow got in and started the car, turning west towards the station.

## SEVENTEEN

As the hour ticked past midnight, Harlow entered the station and found himself greeted at the door by an animated chief Stammerwood. He was holding a wedge of files, looked flustered and out of breath.

"You okay, chief?" Harlow asked.

"Where the hell have you been?"

"We went from the second crime scene to the morgue to have a chat with Donnie. Thought we'd see if he had noticed anything unusual on the first couple of bodies that came in. Why?"

"We're in deep shit with all these bodies."

"Tell me something we don't know, chief."

"No. Look."

Stammerwood grabbed a paper out from between the files he was holding and thrust it into Harlow's hand. Harlow opened it up and read the date in the top right corner, noticing that it was today's copy of the Chicago Tribune.

"Hot off the press, huh?" Harlow said.

"Just read it," Stammerwood replied.

On the front page, the headline of *The Rose Killer Returns* stood out in bold letters. Harlow scanned the article, which detailed how bodies had been turning up for the last couple of days, bearing the same signs as the Rose Killer's victims. Reading on, it claimed that six bodies had turned up in one night, and that it seemed no girl would be safe from the serial killer. The police had no leads and could not seemingly catch the killer. As Harlow continued to read, his name jumped off the page at him. Thankfully it was nothing incriminating, just that: *Detective Harlow, the officer that had been in charge of the investigation for the past three years, refused to comment on the spat of recent murders.* When he reached the bottom of the page, he saw who had written the article.

Stan Markson.

"That bastard," he said through gritted teeth.

"My words exactly," Stammerwood said, snatching the paper out of Harlow's hands. "I've already had a call from the commissioner asking what the hell's going on. He wants it dealt with yesterday. Tell me you've got something from all of this?"

"Well…" Harlow started.

"Do not *well* me, detective. Did I not make myself clear that it will be both our asses if this guy is not caught?"

"You did."

"So what are you doing about it? In the past forty-eight hours, this guy has given us no less than eight bodies. That is almost half of his total body count in the last three years. What the hell is he doing?"

"He likes the attention," Harlow said casually.

"Well, don't we all. That doesn't mean I need to go out there and kill innocent people to get it."

"No, but *he* does. The spotlight has been off him for the past eight months. He's probably been planning this whole scenario, just waiting for the right time to execute it. He would've known that we wouldn't have looked at him for a while, what with all the other cases and police work we have. So, he devised the most extravagant plan he could, to make sure that he would not be forgotten, that he would be in the headlines for a while, and talked about in police departments for years to come."

"That doesn't make any of this more bearable, detective."

"I didn't say it did. The scenes have all been the same. There have been no mistakes, and no faltering on his behalf at all, other than he was early. When he called me, he said twenty-four hours. Well, within nine hours we started to get the call about other bodies appearing. Here we are, twelve hours after the girl from the park, and we have another six bodies. That's the part I don't get."

"It doesn't matter if you get it or not. What matters is catching this guy and getting him off of my streets." Stammerwood's face had gone a deep shade of red with anger, and spittle was starting to come out of his mouth as he spoke.

"We have a couple of leads, chief. We popped back here to see how the guys fared with going to the families and identifying the victims from tonight."

"In your honest opinions, do you think any more bodies are going to be called in tonight?" Stammerwood asked, his voice returning to a normal level.

"My gut feeling tells me no, but it doesn't mean I can't be wrong. I think he's done for the day."

"Lets hope you're right."

Harlow stepped around Stammerwood, who seemed to be frozen to the spot. When he reached his desk and sat down, Garroway said. "We don't have any leads, Ian. Why did you lie to the chief?"

"To get him off our backs. We've got enough shit going on without him breathing down our necks for having nothing on this guy. Can you check in with the uniforms you sent off to the families? I wasn't lying about that. Hopefully they'll have some pictures so that we can tie the girls to a name."

Garroway turned on his heels and headed back out of the door. Harlow sat down in his chair and rubbed his eyes with the palms of his hands. He was tired, angry, and wanted to catch this guy. He got up and headed for the door.

"Where are you going?" Stammerwood barked.

"To get some sleep."

"You have a night like tonight and you're going to get some sleep? Are you *kidding* me?"

"Chief, I've had about four hours worth of sleep in the last few days. I'm running on empty. Now, when I get home I may not end up sleeping but at the very least I'm gonna try. I'll be back in first thing to carry on."

Harlow turned and pushed his way through the doors, despite hearing the chief's raised voice barking something at him as he left. He got into his car and headed for the sanctum of his home.

## EIGHTEEN

As the daylight started to penetrate through the gaps in his curtains, Harlow decided to get up. He looked at his watch; just after six a.m. He'd been awake and staring at the ceiling for the last few hours now. Despite the want of sleep, it had eluded him. Thoughts of the night just swirled in his mind, playing games with him like a cat trying to catch a piece of string.

He showered, put on a clean suit, and headed into the office. When he got to his desk, he noticed a note from Garroway.

*Ian, here are the names and addresses of the victims. When I get in I'll head down to the morgue with you and we'll put the names to the bodies. Charlie.*

It was another full hour before Garroway strode into the precinct. He was clean-shaven - something Harlow had not done for four days now, the stubble was beginning to itch - and had a wide smile on his face.

"What are you so happy about?" Harlow asked.

"I got some sleep and I feel fresh. Don't you feel better for some sleep?"

"I hardly slept, so not really. You ready to hit the morgue?"

"They don't get in for another half hour, Ian, you know that. Anything else come up whilst I've not been here?"

"Nah. I've only been here an hour myself. I got your note, I recognise two of the girls in the pictures from the bodies that we went to yesterday."

"Yeah me too. That's why they were the top two on the pile. My guess is the others will match up to the bodies in the morgue."

Harlow agreed as he shuffled through the pictures for the fifth time that morning. He couldn't believe that such beautiful girls had been taken in their prime, killed for what could only be classed as 'sport'.

Twenty minutes later, the two detectives were in the car and heading for the morgue. Garroway had grabbed a file and placed the pictures within it. As they pulled up outside, they saw Donnie getting out of his own car and walking towards the entrance.

"Morning, Donnie!" Harlow called as he exited the car and placed the fedora on his head.

Donnie turned, and seeing who it was, half-smiled before turning away and continuing towards the entrance. When the two men caught up with him, Harlow asked, "Did you get the rest of the bodies in last night?"

"Yeah," was his simple response.

"Did you manage to get anything from them?"

"Detective," he said, spinning round and exhaling. "It was

a late night for me with the amount of bodies that came in. Can I please get into my office before you start firing questions at me?"

"I thought you liked having all these bodies to play with?" he said, with a hint of sarcasm in his voice.

Donnie swivelled, walked through the doors, and entered the morgue. Garroway smiled but shook his head at the same time at his partner. Harlow shrugged and pulled the door open, allowing Garroway to step in first.

When they were inside the smell of disinfectant hit them. Despite the regular visits and trips, the smell always surprised them. They walked down the dull corridor, pushed the double doors open and stepped into Donnie's 'office'.

They'd not been far behind him, but Donnie was already out of his coat and into a long blue gown. He was putting on a pair of gloves, poking at one of the bodies. Garroway placed the file down onto one of the tables and opened it, pulling the Polaroids from within, and spreading them across the table top.

"We've got some names for them," he said.

Donnie stopped what he was doing and glanced over at the pictures. It obviously interested him as he walked over and looked at the pictures on the table. He picked up one and walked across the room, placed it onto a body beneath a sheet, and moved back to the table. He walked back and forth with one picture at a time, placing each onto a body.

"There you go," he said, and walked back over to the first body he was looking at.

Harlow and Garroway walked the room, which had a body on each autopsy table. They now had a picture atop of the sheets, indicting who was who.

"Our first body from last night was Vicky Connor. Next up was Victoria Spencer, but we knew that one," Harlow said.

"The rest were Jane Ranston, Rebecca Cumin, Alison Hayes, and Claire Layman," Garroway said as he walked around the room, looking at the pictures on the other bodies.

Harlow pulled a cigarette out of the packet and put it in his mouth. As he struck a match to light it, Donnie barked. "There is no smoking in here, detective Harlow!"

Harlow shook the match, extinguishing it.

"Sorry," he said. "Is there anything odd or out of the ordinary that you've come up with since looking at the bodies?"

"Not really. It's odd and out of the ordinary that so many bodies appear in one night, but I guess that's not the kind of thing you were after."

"Help me out here, Donnie. I need to catch this guy. Has he slipped up anywhere?"

Donnie exhaled loudly.

"You know if you give me something, we'll get out of your hair and leave you in peace with this lot."

Donnie paused for a moment; his face had a thoughtful look about it.

"There is something I've noticed on two of the bodies so far. It may be on more but I've not gone through all of them yet."

"What have you found, Donnie?"

"I was going to wait until everything was done. Publish it in the reports and when you read them you would've seen."

"Time is of the essence here, Donnie. Who knows how many more girls this fucker has lined up. Have you got anything that might lead us in his direction?"

"Well," he said slowly. "It might be nothing."

"It might be *everything*," Harlow prompted.

"Under the fingernails of two of the girls, I found some dirt."

"What does that mean?"

"Well, from the look of them they don't strike me as being the hands that suit that kind of women. You know out in the garden or getting dirty, playing in the dirt, stuff like that?"

Harlow glanced round the room at the bodies and thought for a moment, about the women he had seen that had been victims of the Rose Killer.

"You're right," he said. "They are all very well kept women. They look like they take pride in themselves."

"Exactly," Donnie agreed. "Well, the dirt that I found under the fingernails wasn't the only thing. Their clothes seemed to have a bit of a distinctive smell. I wouldn't have thought anything of it had it only been on one of the girls but as it has been on two so far, it seemed a bit strange."

"What kind of smell?" Harlow asked.

"A very distinct fish smell."

Harlow looked across at Garroway, whose eyes were widening with every word spoken.

"The sonofabitch," Harlow said.

"We might have been close," Garroway said.

"Am I missing something, detectives?" Donnie asked.

"If we carried on our search we might have found him," Harlow said ignoring Donnie's question.

"We need to get back out there, Ian."

"Agreed. Thanks Donnie. Let us know if anything else comes up."

Harlow placed his hat back on his head and the two detectives walked out of the morgue, leaving Donnie staring into the space they'd just vacated, wondering what had just happened.

They arrived back at the car, jumped in, started it up and roared down the road towards the warehouses.

"You really think he's going to be there?" Garroway asked.

"There's only one way to find out."

"Surely it won't be that easy?"

"Nothing will be easy, but he's getting sloppy now. He rushed the girls last night. Maybe it was a bigger job than he thought it would be. If there was dirt under the nails, it suggests to me that they could have tried getting away. Or it might be that they were dragged through the dirt after being drugged."

"We've got him now," Garroway said, smiling.

"Don't get cocky yet. There are a number of warehouses by the waterfront that he could be in. I'll drop you where we left off the other day, and then I'll circle round and work my way down from the top. We will probably meet in the middle. We'll both take a walkie. If you find anything, then call."

Garroway nodded, although Harlow didn't see this as he was focused on the road before him.

"Okay?" He asked.

"Yeah."

## NINETEEN

The Mainline screeched around the bend and Harlow steered it onto the gravel, as they neared the warehouses. He slowly stopped, pulling the car to the same spot as the previous day.

"You gonna be okay?" he said, as Garroway was getting out of the car.

"Don't worry about me. Let's just catch this fucker."

Garroway shut the door, and headed away towards the warehouses opposite. Harlow put his foot down on the gas, gravel spraying out from underneath the car as the tyres tried to find some traction. He drove north along the water, the buildings on his right flying by. When he reached the top of the estate he slowed, and brought the car down to a more manageable pace.

He turned at the end and slowly started to trace his way south. The first four warehouses were all still in use. He knew that if the warehouse was in use, there's no way that The Rose Killer could be using it to stash the women.

The next one, however, looked empty. He stopped the car, pulled his Colt out of the holster, and flicked the chamber out to see that it was fully loaded. Then with a flick of the wrist, the chamber snapped back into place. He kept the weapon in his right hand, and grabbing the flashlight out of the glove box, stepped out of the car.

He tried the handle on the first warehouse; it moved and he pulled the door open. The metal wheels squealed as they were moved. When the door was open enough for him to get through, he stepped inside and clicked the flashlight on. He scanned the warehouse, seeing nothing but empty wooden crates turned on their sides. He exited and moved on.

The next two were also open, and empty. The fourth and fifth in the row were being used for various operations. The next was empty. The seventh warehouse Harlow got to was out of use. He tried the door but it didn't move, he wiped the sweat from his brow with the sleeve of his coat and yanked hard on the lever again. No movement. It was the first door in the run that wasn't unlocked. He walked towards the right side of the building and turned the corner.

In front of him was a dark coloured Buick LeSabre. It looked a lot like the one he had noticed a couple of times at the crime scenes, and outside of the morgue. He clicked the flashlight on and shone it through the window, lighting up the interior as he flicked it from front to back. The car was empty, no sign that it was even in use. He walked back and placed his hand on the bonnet; it felt warm.

*Either someone takes really good care of their car, or it's just a coincidence,* he thought.

Harlow walked down the side of the building. In between all of the brickwork stood a solitary white door. He tried the handle, it didn't move. Slightly further down there was window; he reached it and cupped both hands around his eyes, trying to see inside. The grime on the outside prevented him from seeing within. He rubbed the pane with the sleeve of his coat but all it did was smear the grime further. Harlow turned and scanned the floor, looking for something to use. His eyes landed on a flat piece of metal, which looked like it had belonged to part of a crate at some point. He picked it up, paused, and slid it underneath the window. He put pressure on his end and the window moved upwards slightly. He pushed a bit harder and it raised further up. He got his hands beneath and pushed the window the rest of the way up.

The smell of the fish hit him full in the face, causing him to turn away and take a few deep breaths. He stuck the flashlight through the now open window and scanned slowly. A lone desk lay unused in the centre of the room, but other than that, it was empty.

He slipped the flashlight into his pocket and using both hands, hoisted himself off the floor and up and through the window. Retrieving the flashlight from his pocket, he continued to search the room.

The desk proved to be the only thing in there. He opened the drawers but they were empty. He turned the flashlight off and walked over to the door of the room.

Harlow crouched and slowly turned the handle, which moved, until the doorjamb had come out of its lock. He eased it open, and then let go again. He pulled the door ajar and stayed completely still, listening.

Thirty seconds passed.

Confident that no one had heard him, he opened the door enough to be able to get through. His eyes had adjusted to the darkness now and he could see outlines of several shapes.

This warehouse wasn't empty.

He stepped out into the space and eased to a stop. He wanted to turn on the flashlight so that he could see, but did not want to risk anyone, if indeed there was anyone in there, seeing him. He didn't want to be made.

A full minute passed before he took another step; during that time, his eyes kept adjusting, making out a few more shapes. He could now see stacks of boxes in piles around the vast space. He wasn't sure how many there were but it was obvious that there were quite a few. Just as he reached for his pocket, he noticed a dull glow formed around the outside of one of the stacks.

He took a step forward and craned his head around it. There was a small light emitting from the other side of the warehouse.

He pulled his gun out of the holster, and took a step over to the stack before him. The smell of fish increased tenfold, so he raised his coat to cover his nose.

When Harlow finally got used to the harsh smell, he crouched down behind the crates and listened.

Nothing.

He peered round the corner, towards the light. It was coming from a slight crack in a door that was on the other side of the warehouse.

He moved from one stack to another, slowly getting himself closer to the door. As he reached the last one he stopped again, listening for any sounds.

Still, there was nothing.

He reached the door and peered through the crack. The light was harsh on his eyes after the darkness, and he moved away for a moment blinking furiously.

He slowly pushed the door open until he could fit, and squeezed through the gap into the room. With his weapon up, he panned left and right.

All clear.

The light came from a dull bulb, which hung from the ceiling, flickering every now and then, clearly on its last legs. He'd stepped into a small corridor. It was unusual for warehouses to contain interior rooms, so the fact this one did puzzled him. He stepped to the door at the end of the small corridor, and placed an ear against it.

No noise.

He placed his hand on the handle and slowly turned it.

It was unlocked.

As the lock came out of the latch, Harlow swung it open and, in one movement, followed through into the room with his gun up once more.

This one was not empty.

The dull light from the corridor illuminated the small room. There was a desk in the corner with a chair pulled up next to it, another door on the far left side, and one more thing; a bucket.

Harlow walked over to it and clicked on his flashlight. Within the bucket, he counted eleven long stemmed red roses sitting in a pool of water. He quickly went over to the desk and shone the light over it. On the surface there sat a typewriter, but no paper fed onto its roll. Harlow opened the drawer and found a couple of envelopes; one of them had his name on it. He turned it over and opened it but there was nothing inside.

*Clearly not written it for me yet,* he thought.

He turned and went to the other door in the room. He went through in the same style he had done to the previous rooms, and noticed this one was very different. On either side of the room, there were two rows of bunk beds, four per side. The one closest to the door had someone in it.

He approached cautiously, his gun unwavering, pointing at the bed. When he got alongside it he saw that the person within was a woman.

She had blonde hair.

Harlow tilted his head and looked at her face. She looked

to be in her late twenties. He put two fingers on her neck, just below her jawline on the left side. He breathed a sigh of relief as he felt the thud of a weak pulse. He shook the girl slightly.

"Hello? Ma'am? Can you hear me?"

Nothing. He shook slightly harder.

"Chicago PD. Hello?"

Still nothing. He moved his hand away from her and reached for his radio. As he did, he heard a click come from behind him and felt something hard and cold push into the back of his head.

# TWENTY

"Take your hand away from the radio, detective."

Harlow didn't recognise the voice, but slowly did what he was told.

"Good. Now put your gun down on the ground."

The voice was calm, authoritative.

Harlow once again obeyed the order.

"Good. Now keep your hands where I can see them. We wouldn't want you getting any silly ideas now, would we?"

Harlow was desperate to turn round. He wanted to see the face, see who had been killing all of these women. He moved his head slightly to one side.

"Ah ah, stay where you are," the voice said. "I was hoping we would meet under slightly different circumstances to this, detective."

"I hoped I'd catch you in the act, but this is as good as it can be I guess," he growled.

"You've got nothing, detective. You're on your own if you hadn't noticed? *If* you get out of here and call for back up, I'll be long gone, with no trace of my presence by the time they get here. Then you're back to square one."

"If I get out of here, it will be with you in handcuffs."

"You're so confident for someone that's not in a great position. Now. Down on your knees."

Harlow slowly started to sink down to his knees. He was helped by a shove in the back. His knees hit the cold hard surface with a thud. The anger was beginning to rise.

"You're a sick fuck," he said.

"Detective! I'm *appalled* at your language. You didn't speak to me like that the last time we met. Although, when that happened, you did catch me unawares. How is the shoulder by the way?"

Harlow could sense a hint of a smile as those last words were spoken.

"It's fine. Thanks for your concern."

"Good. Now, what to do with you, detective? You came in here just as I was about to take this young lady out on the town."

Harlow's eyes flicked across to the unconscious girl on the bed.

"Yes, you tend to arrive at the most inconvenient of times."

He heard a couple of footsteps from behind him as the killer edged closer. He felt a hand reach down, inside of his coat. Harlow could feel the killer's breath near his ear. It took every ounce of strength not to turn round and rip the guy's head off. As it stood, he knew he would be heavily at a disadvantage. The hand emerged from the coat with his handcuffs. He felt one clasped onto his right hand and wobbled as the killer dragged the limb across to the left.

*It's now or never,* he thought.

He swivelled on the spot, bringing his left hand round in a closed fist, and caught the killer flush in the cheek. The killer rocked back, clearly surprised by the blow. Harlow followed it up with another punch to the killer's face. The killer dropped to the floor, holding the side of his head. Harlow was now standing up and over the person that he'd been chasing for the last three years, the person that had killed twenty-five women, and would have killed a twenty-sixth if it wasn't for his intervention now.

The person that lay on the floor before him didn't look like anything special. He had a black overcoat on over the top of a grey shirt and black tie. He had a black hat on his head, pulled low covering his face. Harlow leant down and took the hat off. As he did, the killer punched him square in the chest. The wind escaped Harlow's lungs and he staggered back. The killer stood up and advanced. He came with confidence and speed. He punched Harlow in the side of the head, and Harlow went down on one knee. As he tried standing, the killer kicked him back to the floor and then punted him in the ribs. Harlow curled up as another boot came his way.

"*I didn't spend all of these years on my craft for it to finish like this!*" The killer spat at Harlow.

Harlow couldn't respond, he was desperately trying to get the air back into his lungs, to recover.

"Why…" Harlow rasped, but couldn't get enough air in to finish the sentence.

"Why what?"

"Why…" Harlow tried again, sucking in as much air as he could.

"What's wrong with you? Can't talk all of a sudden?"

The killer crouched down next to Harlow. As he reached out to grab the detective, Harlow mustered all of the energy that he could and swung his left fist off the ground, and connected with the killer's nose. The crunch as the nose broke was sickening in the silence of the room.

The killer fell backwards, clutching his nose, blood

streaming down his face. Harlow dragged himself off the floor and booted the killer, who now mirrored how Harlow had looked moments ago. He reached into his coat pocket and pulled out a small key. He put it into the handcuff that was still attached to his right wrist and turned it. There was a snick as the lock came undone. Harlow walked over, punched the killer in the side of the head once more, and then positioned his hands behind his back, cuffing him as he went. The killer rocked up into a sitting position, and stared up and Harlow.

There were darkening streaks of blood cascading down his face. His eyes looked as black as anything Harlow had ever seen before, almost lifeless. He looked to be in his mid-thirties, to Harlow anyway, and there was nothing distinguishing about him. If you saw him on the street, you wouldn't have even looked twice in his direction.

Harlow read him his Miranda rights. During the process, the killer stared straight at him, almost looking through the detective. Harlow then frisked the killer but found every pocket to be empty.

"You gonna tell me your name?" Harlow said, pulling the pack of cigarettes out of his pocket.

"You know my name," the killer said, with a wry smile. "They call me The Rose Killer, don't they?"

"Your real name."

"I didn't ask for that name. Although, I thought it had a catchy ring to it so I stuck with it. Did you not get my letters?"

"Of course I did, but that's not your name."

Harlow struck a match and lit the cigarette, taking a long pull on it before waving his hand to extinguish it.

"Smoking will kill you, detective. Did nobody teach you that?"

Harlow took a step forward, crouched slightly, and punched the killer hard in the chest, causing him to double over. To the annoyance of the detective, he could hear the killer laughing.

"You think that's funny?" he said as he punched him again, harder this time.

The laugh intensified and Harlow hit him again, and again. The laughter continued. He stood up and walked towards the door.

"Where...where are you going?" The killer asked, in between laughing and struggling to breath. "I thought we were having fun?"

"Fun? How is this fun? You're a sick freak."

"No, detective. I'm just full of vengeance, which I am letting out."

"Vengeance? Vengeance for what?"

"For being mistreated."

"When?"

"Oh, many years ago now. I was a mere young adult. Had the love of my life and everything. We were high school sweethearts. We fell in love and planned to get married. Everything was perfect. Of course, that was until she left me."

Harlow stared at the killer as he recounted the story.

"She claimed she loved me but she liked someone else, had met him a couple of times, and realised that she preferred him. That is where my vengeance comes from, detective."

"I'm sure she wouldn't take kindly to you killing all of these women."

"Maybe. Maybe not. Who knows?"

"Did you try talking to her? Try getting her back?"

"Of course I did. She wasn't interested. She moved on very quickly, it seems."

"When was the last time you tried talking to her?"

"Right before I killed her."

The words hung in the air for a moment. The killer stared into Harlow's eyes, not moving. No reaction on his face but a slight smile at the corners of his mouth.

"You killed her?"

"She was my first," the killer said proudly.

"Then why keep going?"

"Because it seemed that all of the women that I killed had the same thing in common. The one thing your department, and you, failed to see."

"Which was?"

"They all fucked their boyfriends or husbands over, one way or another. All of those dirty blonde whores deserved what they got."

There was so much hatred in the words now that Harlow almost thought he was talking to a different man.

"So you thought it was your right to put them in their place?"

"If you are insinuating that their place is in the ground, then yes." The calmness returned.

"I wasn't insinuating anything. You were. One thing I don't get though. Why kill the person that broke your heart? Surely that didn't fix anything."

"It put my mind at ease. She broke my heart, so I stopped hers from beating. I felt that was a fair trade."

"Far from a fair trade. Do you not think that you put the person that was with her through the same kind of heartache by taking her away? You probably broke up a happy home."

"You tell me, detective. Did I break up a happy home?"

Harlow tilted his head slightly taking the information in. There was silence for a full minute before he spoke.

"What do you mean by that?" he eventually said.

The killer stared up at him with a smile beaming across his face.

"Did I break up a happy home? Was *your* home happy, detective?"

Harlow's eyes darted right and left as he tried to comprehend what was being said to him. He closed his eyes for a moment, and thought back to the day he had come home, to find his wife dead in the kitchen.

Her face battered.

Her arm broken.

Strangled to death.

"You!" Harlow shouted.

The killer said nothing, just nodded, the smile still strong on his face.

"But. I don't..." Harlow struggled to say.

His head was swimming, thoughts ripping through his mind.

"Katherine was *mine*. *You* took her away from me," the killer hissed. "So *I* took her away from *you*."

Harlow leapt across the room landing a punch firmly across the killers face. He rocked backwards onto the floor, and Harlow was on top of him in a flash. He punched him hard in the face, once, twice, three times. Blood was spattering left and right with each blow. As Harlow raised a tired fist to hit him again, his hand was grasped from behind.

"Ian, stop!"

The voice came through clearly. Harlow knew it, but couldn't place it. His head was all over the place. He tried shrugging the hand off to continue the beating, but the arm holding his was strong.

"Ian, stop!" The call came again.

He felt another arm come around him from behind and pull him off the killer. He kicked out with all his might, trying to land one last blow. Despite the blurring in his eyes, he could see that he had made a mess of the man's face. He slouched back onto the floor and glanced upwards. A familiar face came into view, the one of his partner.

"Ian. Can you hear me?"

Harlow shook his head, trying to clear the fog that had descended. The rage still flowed through him, but he felt more in control now.

"Ian. It's me, Charlie. You've got him. No need to do anymore damage."

Harlow could see Garroway glancing over at the mangled mess of the body on the floor. He heard Garroway pick up his radio and call for back up.

"Charlie. Cancel the back up. I need to finish this," Harlow croaked.

"No way, Ian. You've done enough to him," Garroway said gesturing towards the groaning mess on the floor.

"You don't understand..."

"It's okay, Ian. He's got his just desserts. The boys in the jail will have fun with his ass."

Harlow tried to raise himself back up off the floor, but Garroway held him firmly down.

"It's for the best," Garroway said to him.

Harlow could hear sirens in the distance, growing louder. He stared over at the man that he had nearly beaten to death, and thought back to what had been said to him. A tear slowly started to roll down his cheek.

## TWENTY-ONE

As the rain continued to beat against the window, the light of the day started to rise. Harlow stood staring out at the nothingness like he had been doing all night. He'd already gone through a full pack of cigarettes and showed no signs of slowing down.

He hadn't moved for hours, not really staring at anything, or thinking about anything, other than the words uttered by the killer. In his left hand, he held a picture of his former wife, the love of his life, who had been murdered eight years ago. He wondered whether her death gave him the inspiration, the need to catch The Rose Killer so badly. His wife was killed in the same way. Maybe, subconsciously, he knew all along that his wife was a victim of The Rose Killer. Maybe he didn't want to see it. He never knew the name of the person that she had been with before. It didn't really matter to him. All that mattered was that he loved her, and she loved him. They'd been so happy, until she had been taken away from him.

"Katherine was mine, you took her away from me," he said slowly.

He'd repeated the sentence many times throughout the night, to no one but himself. How had he missed it?

There was a knock at the door, startling the detective and dragging him out of his thoughts, kicking and screaming into the real world once more. He stood silently, not moving for a full minute before the knocking came again. He moved slowly away from the window, through the hall, and opened the door.

"Hey, Ian." Garroway said, smiling slightly. "I figured you'd be up."

Harlow said nothing, just turned and walked away, leaving Garroway stood in the doorway. Garroway stepped inside and closed the door behind him. He placed a sopping wet umbrella down by the door and shook his coat off.

"It's horrible out there. Rains not eased up all night. With the damn wind, it hits you in the face no matter which way you turn."

Harlow said nothing.

"Look. The chief wants you to come in to the station. He needs to talk to you about what happened last night. About what was said between you two and what you did to him."

"He fucking deserved it," Harlow hissed.

"I know that, Ian. Hell most of us do, but you've got to come in and talk to the chief. He's going to have to tie up all the loose ends."

Harlow said nothing. Just stared out of the window into the distance once more. Without even thinking about it, he took out and lit another cigarette.

"Ian. You okay?"

It was a stupid question. Garroway knew this as soon as the words left his lips, but it was too late.

"Okay? You're asking if I'm okay. How do you fucking think I am? You find out that the sick bastard that's been out there killing all of those innocent women in the last three years did so because the love of his life left him for you. *And* then he killed your wife as part of that plan. How would you fucking feel?"

"Hey, Ian, look I'm sorry. I'm just worried about you is all. We've been partners for six years. You know if there's anything I can do, I'll do it."

"I know. I'm sorry, Charlie," Harlow said lowering his head, and his voice.

"Come down to the station with me. We'll go in and talk to the chief and get this all straightened out. My guess is that he'll let you have some time off after this anyway."

"I don't want any time off."

"You know what I mean. Some good news, the girl is fine. She had a lot of sleeping tablets in her system. As usual, just enough for her to be out for a long time, but not enough to kill her. The docs are pumping her with some drugs to counter act it as we speak. She should be up and about again in the next couple of days. We'll be able to ask her some questions and see if we can determine what happened to her."

Harlow nodded slowly.

"Come on. I'll give you a ride to the station."

Garroway walked across the room and put his hand on Harlow's arm, moving him away from the window and leading him towards the door. Harlow put the picture of his wife down on the chair as he walked past, and headed out of the door and into the rain.

## TWENTY-TWO

As they pulled up to the station, Garroway turned to his partner and said, "Look, Ian. There's a big buzz in there today because you caught him. None of the guys know about, well … everything else. All they know is that you caught him. Try and be nice when they mob you, okay?"

"I'll try," Harlow responded.

They got out of the car and headed into the station. There was a cacophony of noise from all of the officers. As soon as they saw him, they all stopped and turned towards him. Harlow instinctively stopped and one of the officers started to clap. More joined in and within a few seconds, the station had erupted with clapping from all corners. People started to move towards him, grabbing his hand and shaking it enthusiastically, congratulating him for catching the killer. Harlow had seen this kind of thing before but had never been on the end of it. Garroway eased him through the crowd of people and towards Stammerwood's office.

When they were inside, Garroway shut the door and the noise died away. Stammerwood looked up from the paperwork that he was reading and gestured for them to take a seat.

Both of the men complied, and there was silence for a full thirty seconds.

"So," Stammerwood started. "Firstly I want to congratulate you on a fine job, detective."

Harlow stared at him, but said nothing.

"Secondly, I want to say I'm sorry for the other news. I understand how hard this must be for you."

"Do you?" Harlow spat, angrily interjecting. "You have no fucking idea how hard this is for me, chief."

Stammerwood look stunned at the attack. He blinked quickly trying to get back to his chain of thought. "Normally, I would not accept that attitude, detective. But, given the recent circumstances I will let it slide."

"I don't care what…"

"However," Stammerwood interrupted. "That being said, I will not let it continue."

Silence filled the room again.

A minute passed.

"You need to understand that I have been placed in a very awkward situation here. Yes, we've caught the killer, and you caught him as he was preparing to take another victim onto the street, but the problem I have now is simple; I have a serial killer in critical condition in the hospital."

"It's no more than he deserves. If I had my way he wouldn't be breathing," Harlow growled.

"Well, I guess we should say that we're lucky you didn't get your way then. The doctors assure me that he will pull through. He will then go to trial for the murders of all of those women, and be placed into jail for the rest of his days, or given the death sentence."

"Justice would have been letting me kill him."

"Justice, as you so eloquently put it, will be served in the court of law, and not by your hand. I understand your pain, but I need to try and smooth this over with the commissioner."

"Chief, I don't care what you say or think about me for what I did. If it wasn't for Charlie arriving on the scene when he did, you would have a face with no recognisable features and another dead body in the morgue. What he did to those women, and what he did to me, deserves nothing less than death. If you feel I'm being out of order for saying that, then take my badge."

Harlow unclipped his badge and chucked it across the desk. It settled in front of Stammerwood, who just stared down at it not knowing what to say or do. Harlow slowly got to his feet. He looked at Garroway and nodded once. As he reached the door, Stammerwood spoke.

"Detective. Off the record, the fucker got what he deserved. In my opinion, he should also be dead. However, I can't say that on the record. I don't blame you for doing what you did. I'm glad you caught him and got him off the streets. Take your badge."

He tossed the badge back at Harlow, who caught it. He ran his fingers across the metal of the badge, feeling all of the indents and bobbles on the metal.

"It's funny," he said. "When I took this job, Katherine told me that I'd be catching the bad guys now, but it's because of me that we had one of the worst ones out there."

He shook his head slightly.

"Harlow, I don't want you thinking that. You're one of my best, always have been and probably always will be. Right now, you need to find yourself and you'll come back stronger from this. I have no doubt about that."

"Thanks, chief. I think I need to be out of the way of the precinct for a while. Might take a little time off, if that's okay with you?"

"I thought you said…" Garroway started.

"I know what I said, Charlie. I think I need to clear my head. No point being clouded all the time."

"That's fine, detective. One more thing before you go."

Harlow stood, poised with his hand on the handle of the door.

"We know who he is. His name is Daniel Gabdon."

Harlow nodded.

"At least we can stop calling him the fucking Rose Killer now, I guess."

He grabbed he handle of the door and headed back out into the noise of the station, before exiting the building.

## TWENTY-THREE

There was a loud buzz and a click as the door unlocked. Harlow stood in the entrance and glanced at the guard on his right, who nodded before stepping through. The room was a dull grey, just like the rest of the building. The only item within it was a grey table. On a seat, beside the table, was Daniel Gabdon.

His hands were cuffed and chained around a loop on the floor. Harlow stepped to the table, grabbed the other chair and sat down. Gabdon's head and face were a mass of cuts and scars. His nose was disjointed from when it had been broken. He looked up from the table, and smiled when he saw the detective.

"I wondered if you'd ever come," he said.

"I thought I'd let your face heal before I came to question you."

"My face is of no interest to you. You made that very clear when we last met."

"Indeed. Well, you were lucky my partner intervened when he did."

"What would you have done, *detective*?"

"Unfortunately for us both, you will never know the answer to that question."

"Why have you waited for three weeks before coming to see me? Could you not face me? Did what I tell you grind at you too much?"

Harlow ignored the comment.

"I have a few questions for you regarding…"

"I've answered all the questions that your fellow detectives have asked of me. I have confessed to the murders of all of those women, and explained in great detail why I did what I did. You will already know this. So *why*, detective, are you here?"

Harlow paused before answering.

"Surely there is something bothering you? Something you want to know the answer to? Maybe it's a personal thing? Something that the other detectives didn't ask me? Now let me see, what could it be?"

Gabdon gazed upwards, seemingly in thought.

"I have a few questions," repeated Harlow.

"I'm all ears."

Gabdon made a gesture with his hands, motioning for Harlow to continue.

"I want to know why Katherine's leaving you turned you psychotic?"

"Not holding back I see."

"You don't want me to beat around the bush, so I'm getting right to the point."

"I like that, detective. Now, lets see. Why did Katherine leaving me make me psychotic?"

He played on the question a couple of times before looking at the detective, dead in the eyes.

"She broke my heart. I broke her. She didn't make me what I am, just helped release it. I had moments whilst with her where I wanted to hurt people, not women you understand, just people that annoyed me, but I always managed to reign myself in because she calmed me. When she wasn't there anymore, lets just say there was no one there to try and make me stop."

"Why did you kill all of those…?"

"Do you want to know what she said to me right before I killed her?" Gabdon interrupted.

Harlow clenched both of his fists and released them again.

"You want to hurt me don't you? I don't blame you. I'd want to hurt me too."

"Your lucky you're still breathing," Harlow growled.

"I'm not sure luck has anything to do with it, detective. I'm still breathing because you didn't finish the job. However, you didn't answer my question. Do you want to know what she said to me right before I killed her?"

"No."

"Too bad. I think I'll tell you anyway…"

"Shut your mouth," Harlow shouted.

"You have a real bad temper, detective, you know that?"

"As far as I'm concerned, every time you open your mouth a lie comes out. No matter what you say to me or what you claim to know, I don't believe you."

"What reason have I ever given you to not believe what I have told you?"

Silence ran over the room for a moment.

"She begged for her life," he hissed.

"I told you to shut up."

"She told me she'd come back to me."

"Shut up!"

"She told me she would do anything…"

Harlow raised up off the chair, which fell to the floor

behind him, and raced around the table. He grabbed a hold of Gabdon's prison suit with one hand and held his other in a clenched fist up in the air. He stayed like that for a few seconds. He heard the loud buzz of the door and the click as it opened. Raised voices were coming from behind him as wardens entered the room.

"It's okay," he said. "I'm okay."

He lowered his fist and let go of Gabdon. He felt one of the warden's hands on his shoulder, moving him away.

"Honestly, I'm fine. A moment of weakness was all."

He looked round at the warden who was staring hard at him. The warden shot a glance to his companion, and then looked back at Harlow.

"Honestly, I'm okay."

The warden let go and looked over at the guy by the door. When Harlow looked over at him he could see that he had a truncheon out ready to use if needed.

"If this questioning continues, then I will get Jones to stay in here with you. No more of what just happened. This is your one and only warning. Do I make myself clear?"

"Very," Harlow said, as he walked over and picked the chair back up from the floor.

The second guard left the room and the other, who was obviously Jones, walked over and stood by the door with his arms crossed.

"I told you your temper was bad," Gabdon taunted.

"Believe me when I tell you that there is nothing more I would like to do than smash your face into pieces right now. But I like that you will suffer in here, waiting for your death sentence."

Gabdon shrugged his shoulders.

"I achieved more than I ever set out to do. The ones in the last few days were more of a sport than anything else."

"You're sick. You know that?"

"You call me sick. Other people call me different things."

"What do you call yourself?"

Gabdon thought for a moment, staring off to the side.

"A merchant of vengeance," he said, a gleam in his eyes.

"I want to know why you left roses at the scenes of the girls you murdered."

"They were Katherine's favourite flower. Surely you knew that?"

Harlow clenched his jaw slightly as the comment passed over him.

"So why not leave them on the girls that you shot?"

"Those sluts got shot because they didn't go along with the plan. If they'd played ball like the others, they would have been killed with dignity."

"You call strangling someone 'being killed with dignity'?"

"There's nothing personal about shooting someone. Anyone could do it. The homeless guy on the corner. Little Jimmy grabbing a gun from his dad's cabinet. It's just point and pull the trigger. It becomes personal when you are up close, choking the life out of someone, and looking into their eyes, knowing the last thing they will see is your smiling face."

"Again, you're sick."

Gabdon shrugged his shoulders once more.

"Why did you not leave a rose on Katherine's body?"

He grimaced as he said it, every muscle in his body flinching in a twitch of pain.

The smile widened on Gabdon's face.

"I gave her a rose eventually. I guess that you saw the one on the grave?"

Harlow nodded.

"I didn't know at the time that it would become something I wanted to continue doing. When I killed her, it was for revenge. After I did it I had a wonderful feeling rush over me. I waited a while, thought I would see if I was caught. When I didn't, I decided to kill another, and then another. There are probably about six other murders that I committed, which you never attributed to me. Once I got a feel for it, and knew I wouldn't be caught, I started to leave a rose on the bodies as a sign of respect to Katherine."

"Respect? To the person you *murdered!*"

Gabdon's face twisted slightly at those words.

"Respect to the one I *loved*," he eventually said.

It took every ounce of strength for Harlow not to leap out of his chair and across the table at him. He could sense Jones behind him shift slightly, ready to intervene if anything were to happen.

"Why did you let me live the day, when I almost caught you?" Harlow managed to say calmly.

"I wasn't ready to kill you then. First, I needed you to suffer some more."

"So why the letters?"

"I felt that I'd done everything I could. I wanted us to meet again, and for you to know the truth. I didn't expect to see you when I did, but it all worked out in the end."

"You wanted to be in here? To be up for a death sentence?"

"No. I wanted to see your face when I told you that I killed your wife."

Harlow rubbed his eyes with his hands, taking the time to calm himself down.

"I do have one last question," he said, looking back at Gabdon.

"Yes, detective?"

"How did it feel when Katherine told you that she was leaving you?"

Gabdon looked around for a minute, taking his time before answering. His face dropped as the memories came flooding back.

"Like someone had ripped my heart out and crushed it in front of me," he said slowly.

"Good. That's what I want you to think about every day now, until you die."

Harlow rose from the chair and turned to face Jones. He nodded and the guard knocked on the door. The loud buzzer went off and the door opened. Harlow stepped through without looking back.

## TWENTY-FOUR

Two weeks later, Harlow stepped through the doorway of Stammerwood's office, and sat down on the chair.

"I thought you'd be pleased to hear that Gabdon has been given the death penalty. He will be put in the chair on March 31st. Didn't know if you wanted to be there?"

"No. If I never see him again it will be too soon."

"Why did you go and question him, Harlow? I know that you needed some things answered, but it could've gone wrong. Hell, from what I heard it almost did."

"I had everything under control."

"Hmm. Well, that being said, I'm glad you refrained from doing anything. He's getting what he deserves and we'll make sure it's a painful one."

Harlow nodded and stood up, heading back for the door.

When he left the office, he walked back over to his desk. There was a pile of messages spiked on his desk. He picked the first one up and starting reading it. When he realised that he wasn't concentrating on the words, he put it back on the spike and stood up. Garroway came over and sat down opposite him.

"Leaving already?"

"I got something I need to do."

Harlow grabbed his coat off the rack.

"I heard they are giving Gabdon the chair. Good fucking riddance is what I say."

"Yeah. No less than he deserves."

"You going to watch when they do it?"

"No. I've seen enough of that bastard to last me a life time."

"It'll get easier, Ian. It'll all go away soon enough. You know that right?"

"Yeah. I do. Thanks, Charlie."

He patted his partner on the shoulder and walked through the precinct and out onto the street.

He got into his car and headed north. When he reached the cemetery, he got out and pulled his collar up to shield from the wind and drizzle that whipped in the air. He walked through the graveyard, being respectful to not stand on any graves as he went.

When he arrived at his wife's headstone he bent down and brushed away some of the leaves that had blown over it during the bad weather.

"I'm sorry it's taken so long for me to come," he said. "I've been meaning to for a while now, but have not been sure what to say. I got him in the end. I know that you probably already knew that but I felt I should say it out loud to you."

He paused and looked up into the sky for a few moments, before looking back down again.

"I'm so sorry that it took so long to get him. I never knew that you and him. That he was..."

He struggled with the words. "Well. I'm sorry. Just know that I miss you, and I love you. I always will."

He kissed his fingers and placed them onto the name on the headstone, and held it there for a few moments. Harlow then stood up and turned away, walking back towards his car, and his future.

# THE HIGHWAYMAN

Join Detective Ian Harlow on his next case.

Turn the page to read the first chapter of 'The Highwayman'…

# ONE

**CHICAGO, ILLINOIS**
**MAY, 1955**

Maxine stood on the corner of a dark street, the dull glow of the streetlight above her acting as a spotlight within the surrounding shadows. Her living, despite being illegal, was a living at least. The cigarette she was holding had almost burned down to the filter, the heat beginning to tingle her fingers slightly. She'd paced up and down the same sidewalk for the past couple of hours without getting a sniff of interest. Maxine thought she had gotten a customer earlier until a police car turned into the street and she had to bail.

She had done the same thing now for eight years. It put food on the table for her and her son, Ethan. He always asked where she was going late at night, but 'work' was all she said. He didn't need to know what she actually did. When he got older, he'd work it out.

A gleaming red car pulled up a hundred yards away, snapping her out of her reverie. It sat with its engine idling, like a hooker in a bar. Maxine tilted her head in confusion, trying to gauge what the person inside was doing, the engine the only noise on the drab street.

Maxine hiked up her dress slightly and pulled at her top so that she was showing more of the goods on offer, before sauntering towards the stationary vehicle. Before she got there, the engine roared and the car pulled away, leaving smoke lingering in the air.

Maxine stopped dead in her tracks and dropped her head, throwing her cigarette to the ground. Another missed opportunity. She turned on her heels, her stilettos scraping on the damp ground beneath.

A moment later, she heard the same roar and saw the same car shining its headlights at the other end of the street. It stopped at the corner and the window shimmied down marginally. Smiling, she took off towards it, determined to not let the opportunity pass her by.

As she got nearer, she could see the white wall tyres and the glint of the streetlights in the perfectly polished alloys. When she reached the side of the car, the window moved all the way down, allowing her to see the rich leather interior.

Maxine bent down, her purse tumbling off her shoulder and clipping the door. "Hi, stranger. Looking for some company?" She noticed he was wearing sunglasses, and a cap pulled down over his face. His shirt was pulled tight across his biceps.

The man behind the wheel didn't even look at her. He nodded slowly.

Maxine smiled and pulled the handle of the door. It opened with a smoothness she wasn't used to for cars in this part of town.

"So, what do I call you?" Maxine asked, as she shuffled

herself into the leather seat, feeling the softness against her exposed skin. The door snicked shut perfectly behind her.

The man said nothing, still not even looking at her. He planted his foot on the accelerator and the car shot off down the road, into the darkness beyond.

Maxine gripped the handle on the door of the car, the pressure pushing her back into the seat. Her eyes widened, but her instincts kicked in. "You like it fast then do you, mister?" she purred as she ran her hand up the man's thigh.

He jolted at her touch and the car veered right then left.

Maxine screamed, and gripped hold of the handle once again. "Let me out, you crazy son of a bitch!" she ordered, yelling at him over the roar of the engine.

He composed himself and settled the car back into the rhythm that he'd started with when he'd picked her up. He said nothing but shook his head slowly.

Maxine scrambled around in her purse, desperately trying to find her small pocket knife as the car screeched to a stop, the smell of burning rubber wafting in through the open window.

The man reached across, grabbed Maxine by the scruff of her hair, and smashed her face into the dashboard of the car. Pain exploded behind her eyes and she felt the warm sensation of blood as it trickled down her face. Her head rocked back against the supple leather of the headrest as her vision swam violently. The last thing she remembered was the noise of the roaring engine once again.

# ALSO BY GARY PEARSON

Hopefully you have enjoyed reading this book as much as I did writing it. Being an independent author I ask that you kindly pop onto the website that you purchased this from and write a short review. This not only helps me grow as an author, learning what people did and didn't like, but also enables other people make a choice on whether they'd like to try it to.

Below is a list of other titles that I have released. You will also find these on Amazon.

Detective Ian Harlow:

*The Highwayman*

Alex Sanchez Stories:

*Retribution*

*Breaking Point*

I have also had a few short stories featured in the below anthologies.

Anthology Stories:

*Trapped - Undead Legacy*

*The Box - Kids Volume 1*

*Downward Spiral - A-Z Book 4*

*Downfall - And the World Will Burn: A Dystopian Anthology*

## ABOUT THE AUTHOR

Gary Pearson is an independent author that has released three novellas, and has many more projects in the pipeline. He was born and raised in the South East of England, but now lives in Stafford in the Midlands, with his wife, two kids, and three dogs.

Gary balances having a full time job as an account manager, whilst being a father, and utilises every opportunity that he can to put pen to paper. Having something out there which other people can read and enjoy, helps to fuel his passion for writing stories.

He hopes that you will continue to join him on his adventure.

To learn more about Gary Pearson please go to www.garyipearson.com, or follow him on any of the social media links below.

facebook.com/GaryPearsonAuthor
twitter.com/GaryP04
instagram.com/garypearsonauthor

Printed in Great Britain
by Amazon